W9-AHG-699

No Longer the Property of NOLS

NORTH OLYMPIC
LIBRARY SYSTEM
PORT ANGELES, WA 98362

THE MAN FROM NOWHERE

There could be only one Roger Travis in the New Mexico Territory.

He had lost the woman he loved in an Indian massacre.

He had lost a year of his life in the tropics, trying to forget.

But he'd come back, his grief tampered down, out of sight of the world. No money, no friends, he had only one thing left—his name. And now, someone had stolen that.

At last, Travis was ready to stand up and fight back.

THE MAN FROM NOWHERE

T. T. Flynn

This hardback edition 1999
by Chivers Press
by arrangement with
Golden West Literary Agency

Copyright © 1958 by Thomas Theodore Flynn, Jr.
Copyright © 1958 by Thomas Theodore Flynn, Jr. in the British
Commonwealth
Copyright © renewed 1986 by Thomas B. Flynn, M.D.

All rights reserved

ISBN 0 7540 8058 7

British Library Cataloguing in Publication Data available

Printed and bound in Great Britain by
Redwood Books, Trowbridge, Wiltshire

1

He had learned, finally, that a man without bold plans and high hopes and humor and laughter had nothing, however recklessly he lived.

He was in Costa Rica, drinking the day's first black, bitter coffee, watching the cottony ground mists steam under another rose-and-gold sunrise, when the future suddenly promised all that again. . . . Seventeen days later, still wearing rumpled tropical whites and the old Western hat he had never discarded, and humming a Guatemalan love song, he walked off a rusty little steamer just docked at San Francisco from sweating, fever-ridden ports far south.

A heavy duffel bag rode his left shoulder. Deck winches were rumbling, men shouting; but he did not look back. The rich reek of dried hides and green coffee, of spices and fish came at him. His smile widened. He walked into it with striding eagerness, taking the bracing coolness of the north once more into bronzed skin and hard flesh.

On the rough cobblestones of the wide waterfront street he paused, smiling up at the soaring hills of the city. On Nob Hill, where the new nabobs of the Comstock Lode had built mansions such as the West had never seen, distant windows glinted in the sunshine. An immense dray loaded with huge hogsheads came noisily at him, and only at the last instant did he move a lithe step. The driver was swearing as the heavy Belgian horses and massive wheels clashed by.

A gleaming carriage and team of matched bays going the other way pulled up before the lone figure in white. The coachman gave wry advice from under the jaunty tilt of his high plug hat.

"Them hooligans drivin' the drays'll flatten a man. Better get your saddle horse, mister."

5

The heavy duffel bag thudded on the blue floor-carpet of the open carriage. The stranger eyed the bright brass buttons on the coachman's long black coat and grinned. "First I'll go to the South Bay Bank, Nob Hill style," he stated cheerfully.

"This here's a private carriage, an' no job left for Howie Quist if he's caught haulin' strangers," said the coachman severely. He consulted a thick silver watch. His broad, sunbaked face looked down shrewdly. "Nob Hill style ain't cheap. . . . You got five dollars?"

Chuckling, the stranger stepped into the carriage. The coachman straightened his plug hat, shook the matched bays into a smart trot and spoke over a shoulder. "The look of cattle is on you."

"Two years ago," the stranger admitted, "I sold a ranch in Wyoming."

He sat comfortably back on the soft cushions and watched hacks and buggies, wagons and carriages fill the city streets they entered. The full midtown cacophony and confusion were about them on Montgomery Street when the carriage drew up with a flourish before the impressive stone façade of the South Bay Bank.

The coachman spoke with a trace of pride as his passenger stepped out. "In Texas, I rode on the Palo Duro for Goodnight."

"A long jump from a Palo Duro saddle to a fancy Nob Hill rig," said the stranger as he started into the bank.

From the wide world, strangers had entered the ornate marble-and-gilt banking room of the South Bay Bank. But when the teller in Cage Two glanced at the draft, he suddenly became nervous.

"You forgot to endorse, sir."

"You're looking at it," was the amiable correction.

"Of course . . . One moment, please." The teller left the cage, taking the draft. When he returned, he said politely, "Mr. Campbell, the cashier, will attend to this. He has your draft." And when the bronzed stranger nodded agreeably and walked to the rear of the large banking room, the teller ducked out of the cage again, almost scuttling on some urgent errand.

The half-paneling in the cashier's office was of rubbed dark walnut. Chairs were crafted in black leather. The carpeting was thick. In that cheerless elegance, William Campbell with his compact build, thinning sandy hair and closely trimmed beard watched from the high-backed swivel chair at his desk as the stranger walked in, hat in hand, and said, "I'm Roger Travis."

This was an unusual case, William Campbell sensed immediately. The rumpled white suit and the old wide-brimmed Western hat had an authentic look. The visitor's face, stripped of superfluous flesh, was molded in strong planes under a shock of brown hair which needed a barber. The wide mouth and the full lower lip held upward lines of humor. And the man had a bronzed litheness and a look of far places, of recklessness and boldness, Campbell noted warily as he reached to his desk.

"I'm told that you presented this draft for five hundred dollars against the account of Roger Travis."

"I did," the stranger agreed, smiling.

"Our books," Campbell said with studied politeness, "show that a certificate of deposit was issued to Roger Travis when the account was opened. You have the certificate, of course."

"Lost it," was the amiable reply.

"The signature and endorsement on this draft," Campbell said calmly, "resemble that of Roger Travis in our 'Signature Book.' The five hundred dollars probably would have been paid without question if the ledger balance had covered the amount of this draft."

"Look again," was the cheerful retort. "Two years ago I deposited thirty-two thousand dollars."

Terse now, Campbell said, "The Travis account has a balance of one hundred and three dollars and sixty cents."

"Mistake somewhere."

"The mistake," said Campbell with full brusqueness, "is yours, young man. You're not, of course, Roger Travis. I, personally, am acquainted with Travis. I inspected his credentials and received his certificate of deposit. Furthermore, over a period of time, the bank's lawyers have assisted Travis in the settlement of an estate. We know—"

7

"What estate?" was cut in swiftly, sharply.

Campbell said coldly, "When Travis returned from Central America somewhat less than a year ago, he learned from letters which the bank had been holding for him that an uncle had passed away and he had inherited."

"An uncle in Ohio," the stranger said without hesitation.

"Yes," Campbell said.

"And you people helped collect the inheritance?" The stranger's tone was hardening.

Stiffly, Campbell replied, "Travis requested our assistance. He wrote immediately, of course, to the lawyer in Ohio who had notified him of his uncle's death."

"Didn't Travis go to Ohio and identify himself?"

"It was not necessary," said Campbell shortly. "Travis and the lawyer in Ohio were old friends. I read the correspondence between them. Incidents of long ago were mentioned by both men. The Ohio lawyer was quite satisfied as to the identity of the Roger Travis who was writing to him."

"Incidents of long ago?" the stranger said. He weighed the statement. "I kept a journal for years," he said levelly, "and lost it when I lost my certificate of deposit. This man evidently has my journal and knows a great deal about my past life." And, when Campbell stared without comment, obviously unmoved, the stranger demanded, "How much did the estate amount to?"

"Something over sixty thousand dollars, I believe." Uneasily Campbell watched the visitor prowl to the nearest window. Prowl, Campbell thought, was the word for the lithe, noiseless steps.

Staring out the window, the man slowly said, "Thirty-two thousand dollars deposited two years ago. Over sixty thousand dollars paid in from Ohio . . . and a hundred and three dollars left."

"And sixty cents," Campbell corrected out of meticulous habits.

The visitor prowled back. "Where's the fellow who got it?"

"Roger Travis left San Francisco some two months ago. He hasn't communicated with us."

"And he won't . . . What did he look like?"

"A most pleasant young man," said Campbell curtly. "A

8

thorough gentleman despite an adventurous background. He was well-liked by all who had contact with him."

"Obviously," in the same level tone. "Never mind the gentleman part. Describe him."

"A large man, about thirty, I should say," Campbell recalled. "Hair on the reddish side. A longish face. Very intelligent blue eyes. He dressed well."

"He should have dressed well with the money he got with a few plausible letters to a trusting old family lawyer in Ohio, and smooth talk to the bank here," the stranger said with irony. "Well, what was his story?"

Campbell wished now that he had made an exit, however undignified, while his visitor was at the window. His anger was stirring at the hardening, insistent questions. But when Campbell looked at the stripped, bronzed face, no longer smiling, he continued talking to hold the man and keep him calm until the help that was coming arrived.

"At various times, Travis spoke frankly," Campbell said stiffly. "Two years ago, it seems, Travis rode from his Wyoming ranch to Texas and brought back a trail herd. And found that while he had been gone, his new young wife had been massacred by Indians. The details were rather—"

"Get on with it!" came with such harshness that Campbell winced and glanced helplessly at the door.

"Travis's life, he told me, had been centered in his wife. It had been truly a union of great love. Losing her—and in such a tragic manner—broke Travis. He wanted only to escape from his memories. He sold out for what he could get and banked the money with us and went to Central America, hardly expecting to return. But finally he realized that fleeing from grief was not a cure, and he came back."

The visitor lifted the stained old hat and stared at it. A stony, sad look held his features for a moment. His comment sounded remote.

"He told a good story. All of it the truth—only the wrong man came back and told it. I'm Roger Travis. Friends in Wyoming and Ohio can identify me."

"By letter?" Campbell said.

"In person, if they must come here to San Francisco."

"And who," Campbell asked, "will identify such strangers

9

if they should appear here?" The knock which Campbell had been expecting sounded on the closed door and his relief was great. "Some of the clerks," Campbell said, hardening into his full accustomed authority, "are outside the door with police. I suggest that you go quietly with them."

The visitor half turned to keep the door in sight. His glance at Campbell was almost curious. "You haven't any intention of letting me identify myself? You'll have me locked in jail while the fellow who's stolen my money is out, free and undisturbed?"

"Your claims," said Campbell shortly, "will be investigated."

"While I'm in jail for as long as you care to keep me there? While your lawyers use their bags of tricks to discredit any friend who tries to identify me, and bolster your claim that I'm the thief? Don't tell me your bank, or any bank, will admit almost a hundred thousand dollars was handed to the wrong man."

Again the knuckles rapped on the door. Campbell held his tone firm. "Justice will be done."

"Justice?" The visitor was quiet; too quiet, Campbell sensed. "What sort of justice for a thief who stole another man's name and memories—and all his money?"

"A bank," said Campbell, "is not the place—"

The quiet voice, edged and coldly speculative, demanded, "How much justice for stealing another man's grief? What justice for using the love and agony of a dead girl to impress a whiskered jackass like you and make the stealing easier?"

The knocks became peremptory. Campbell said, "I'm afraid you'll have to—"

The edged voice cut in, "And now you'll jail me—and try to prove me the thief while the real thief gets more time to leave a cold trail!"

Campbell met the man's flinty stare in reluctant fascination. Slowly his hands closed on the arms of his chair. Fearing now for the door to open, Campbell sat in silent anguish, not sure what was going to happen and fearful for it to happen.

2

The stranger's left hand had slipped into the pocket of his white coat. Mutely Campbell gazed at the sharp bulge a gun muzzle made in the side of the pocket. The bronzed stranger was suddenly hard and reckless-looking, plainly capable of any violence.

"We'll walk out to my carriage!"

Campbell exhaled a soft sigh and stood up.

The bronzed stranger was at his side, hand in the coat pocket when Campbell opened the office door. Four clerks, concerned and excited, stared at them. A bulky, uniformed patrolman, his red-veined face flushed and damp from haste, gazed blankly.

The tall stranger, Campbell saw from the corner of his eye, was standing easily beside him, the hand lazily in the coat pocket, an infuriating, humorous smile directed toward the group.

"This is a mistake," Campbell said thickly, and from habit he made it the clerks' mistake.

Campbell stalked past the group into the busy banking room. The tall stranger strolled at his side and chuckled. "You might be dead by now, my pompous friend. Smile for all the nice people."

Campbell felt apoplectic as he bowed, smiled to a matron whose ledger balances rarely fell under a quarter of a million. She would have been affronted if ignored. Tellers in the cages were gazing at them. Derision would spread through the bank, Campbell knew, when the truth of this was revealed.

Outside the bank, a polished carriage with liveried coachman waited at the curb. The stranger gave Campbell a quizzical look. "I suppose," he said, "I've got you on my hands for a time. Get in."

Helplessly Campbell looked at passing pedestrians. They ignored him. Mutely, Campbell dropped on the carriage cushions, and shock struck him.

"Quist!" Campbell blurted.

The red-faced coachman grinned back uncertainly from his high seat. "Fine mornin', sir."

"This," said Campbell thickly, "is the MacLanes' carriage! You're helping this man!"

"Well, now—you might say it was a friendly pick-up, like," said Quist vaguely and uncomfortably.

The bronzed stranger dropped on the seat beside Campbell and laughed. "Drive on, Howie, around the next corner." And when Quist hesitated, the stranger added cheerfully, "You took the money, Howie. Nob Hill style—remember?"

Quist's backward glance weighed the bulge in the stranger's coat pocket. "This," Quist said dubiously as he faced forward, "is gonna learn me, I think."

The sedately rolling carriage turned off Montgomery Street as the stranger asked Campbell a question. "Was a young man named Dick Kilgore mentioned in all this business?"

"Not that I recall," Campbell said stiffly.

The thoughtful eyes estimated Campbell. "This fellow Travis may return. If he does, remember that the wrong man told the right story—and you were jackass enough to believe him."

Campbell's flush heated the roots of his close brown beard. He was hardly aware that a heavy, stained duffel bag on the floor was forcing him to sit awkwardly. Covertly, desperately, he looked on both sides of the street for possible assistance.

A beefy patrolman was strolling leisurely on the opposite walk. Furtively Campbell glanced at the stranger beside him. The man's sinewy hand was coming out of his coat pocket with a straight-stemmed pipe. The pocket now was flat, obviously empty. The derisive truth struck Campbell. *A pipe, not a revolver.* He had walked submissively out of the bank to the threat of a hidden pipe stem, not a gun.

Campbell swallowed, drew a breath and hurled himself out of the carriage. He landed in a running stumble, and reeled off-balance, dangerously close to an oncoming buggy horse. The horse swerved in fright and reared as Campbell's frantic shout broke out under its head.

"Stop them! Stop that carriage! Stop it!"

Quist swiveled around and saw William Campbell stumbling, shouting under the head of the rearing horse. Quist reached instantly for the long buggy whip. The shout that Quist uttered had never been heard from a liveried Nob Hill coachman. It was a mule skinner's bellow, urging the sleek, matched bays into a plunging run.

Leaning forward, plug hat tilted toward an eye, Quist skillfully drove the polished carriage in a weaving rush through the heavy street traffic. At the next corner, Quist's shout and strong hands swung the team, hoofs clashing, carriage careening, into the cross street. . . . And at the next corner Quist made another skidding turn.

The shouting voices and the patrolman's keening whistle were far behind, lost for the moment, when Quist pulled the blowing team into a sedate trot and cast a harried look over his shoulder.

His passenger, riding comfortably on the deep cushions, chuckled. "Howie, that was worth another fiver. If we could come down Market Street every morning like that—"

Acidly, Howie Quist said, "We ain't comin' down any street like that! I try to make an honest dollar—"

"Five dollars," the stranger corrected with amusement.

"Five, then," said Howie Quist bitterly. "An' I find myself helpin' a stranger with a gun kidnap the cashier of the South Bay Bank!"

"What gun?"

Howie Quist stared back at the straight-stemmed pipe his passenger drew from the coat pocket. Howie blinked. "You took old Campbell outa his bank with *that?*"

"Had to use something."

Howie Quist straightened his tall plug hat and held the team in a brisk trot around the next corner. "Who'll believe it?" Howie complained bitterly. "Why'd you have to use anything?"

"You wouldn't believe me."

Grimly, Howie said, "I'm gonna hear it, an' it better be

13

good." He listened to the brief account his passenger gave, and when he was through, Howie whistled softly. "That yarn's too tall for me."

Wryly, his passenger said, "For me, too—but my money's gone."

"My job," said Howie Quist sourly, "is gone. Who'll believe I wasn't helpin' you? I'm halfway in the jug now." When his passenger laughed softly, Howie looked back warily.

"No one would believe you, Howie, if I said you helped me," the bronzed young stranger said cheerfully. "But if you help me get out of town, I'll not have a chance to say anything—"

"Blackmail!" said Howie dourly. When his passenger chuckled again, Howie cautiously inquired, "Where was you minded to head for?"

"My partner was killed in Central America when a rock slide knocked our horses off a cliff trail into the river below," his passenger began. "We'd sent money to his father in New Mexico to buy cattle for us and hold for the increase. That was in my journal, too, which Travis seems to have. He's gotten everything possible of mine here in San Francisco. My guess is he probably headed for New Mexico where my cattle are."

"It's on the way to Texas," Howie said, cheering slightly. After a moment's thought, he added, "I got money in another bank, might be I could get out. They're lookin' now for the MacLanes' carriage, but I got an idea might keep us outa the jug."

Howie drove four more blocks, turning two corners, and pulled up abruptly beside a closed black public hack waiting at the curb.

"Terrance, old friend!" Howie greeted the hack driver with cordial surprise.

A grin of recognition lifted black, drooping mustaches. "Howie, lad! How goes?"

"You'd not believe," Howie said with false heartiness. "That easy Nob Hill job you been wantin' is yours, Terrance. I'm quittin'. Take the MacLanes' carriage home now an' the job's yours."

"Me hack, Howie! How can I?"

14

Without hesitation, Howie answered, "Your stable is on my way. I'll leave the hack for you."

Terrance visibly wavered, tugging at one side of his mustaches. "What about your passenger there?"

"My new partner," said Howie blandly.

" 'Tis a good job," Terrance conceded enviously. "Well— all right."

Howie Quist was downcast as he stood beside the hack with his passenger and watched the MacLanes' gleaming carriage roll away.

"Likely Terrance'll get the job," Howie guessed. "He has a gift of gab." He turned to his new partner. "If there's somethin' else in that bag to wear, you better change in the hack while I'm drivin'. They'll be lookin' for that white suit. I'll stop by my bank an' then my room."

The stranger tossed the heavy duffel bag into the hack. His glance at Howie Quist was quizzical. "Howie, you don't need to do this. We might not get out of San Francisco. If you're caught with me, you are in trouble."

A slow smile came on Howie Quist's broad, weathered face. "Folks know the MacLanes' coachman," he said. "I'm tired of city life anyways, an' I'm curious about this feller you say is you. I'd like to see him."

Thoughtfully, the bronzed stranger said, "He's clever. He's got the money now and he's dangerous. Some way I'll find him, but it might be best for you to keep clear of it."

Howie's grin broadened. "That," Howie said, "I mean to see."

3

A thousand miles east and south of San Francisco, the man who had called himself Roger Travis for months rode leisurely into the busy, sun-drenched plaza of Soledad, in

New Mexico Territory, cheerfully musing on his immense good fortune.

He had been a drifter, seeking money through restless, roving years, and finding it elusive. . . . Until, in a steamy tropical clearing in distant Guatemala, he had found an illiterate native *mozo* discarding the papers of two dead men who had been swept off the trail by a rock slide. The *mozo* and pack mules had escaped.

Satisfied of the story's truth, Travis had gone through the papers. And, in the journal of a dead man's life, a certificate of deposit in a San Francisco bank and other papers, he had found suddenly the fortune he had so long sought. He had the keys to a dead man's life, a dead man's money. All that was needed was the will to gamble boldly. He had gambled and won; now Travis knew that anything was possible.

As he tied his horse to a hitchrack, Travis thought again of the man's young wife who had been massacred by Indians in Wyoming. In the closely written pages of her husband's journal, the young wife had come alive, vivid and real. She had been unafraid and laughing and her arms had been tender. . . . All that and more was written in happiness and agony of grief in the husband's journal. All of it had become his own life now, and he felt no guilt.

A triple hitch of mules and a groaning, high-sided ore wagon rolled heavily through the plaza. Travis lifted a friendly hand to the driver, and then noted a Franciscan priest in belted brown robe and leather sandals also crossing the plaza. Charity, Travis reflected with wry humor, never hurt a man's luck. He was feeling expansive anyway over another bold gamble he had decided to make.

"Padre!" Travis called, and when he reached the priest he said, "Something for your church."

The sun-browned Franciscan regarded the five yellow double eagles which Travis dropped into his palm. "You are generous, Mr. Travis." He had a slight accent.

Travis chuckled. "Do you keep tally on strangers in town?"

The priest's smile came. "The talk of the country comes to church. You are Roger Travis, the partner of young Richard Kilgore when he was killed in Central America.

16

You are visiting the Kilgore ranch and have made many friends already."

"You're Father Philippe," Travis said, chuckling again. "You came here from France four years ago. I heard it in the Bonanza Bar."

Humor spread on Father Philippe's thin face. "I should be talked about more often in such places." He glanced at the gold coins and sobered. "Prayers will be offered for your intentions, Mr. Travis. Is there someone you wish remembered?"

The kindly expectant look on the *padre's* face reminded Travis of the man he was impersonating. "I lost my wife a little over two years ago," he said sadly. It came easily now from his long, intent studies of the husband's journal. "I called her Vicky," Travis said. "Victoria Travis."

"Your Vicky will be remembered," Father Philippe promised. "And God grant all that you deserve." His smile was kindly as he walked on, a slender, serene man, burned by the country.

Travis stood with a peculiar, stricken chill. . . . *God grant all that you deserve!* He had offered the gold coins in a gambler's careless gesture to bolster luck. And the *padre* had left him with an accusing thought which ate in corrosively for a moment, leaving a sense of uneasy portent. With an effort, Travis shook off the chill feeling as he walked on across the plaza to the squat red brick building which housed the Soledad Bank.

Ed Jackson, who ran the bank, was a modest, graying man, slow-talking, and also slow-thinking, Travis had decided scornfully. Jackson's office was in the front of the bank, and when he saw his visitor in the office doorway, Jackson stood up quickly from his desk to shake hands.

Travis dropped into a chair by the desk and balanced his black hat on a knee. He had cultivated Jackson with some care. He was easy and smiling now as he came to the point at once.

"Matt Kilgore tells me his luck turned bad and he borrowed thirteen thousand dollars from the bank, on a note made due and payable ninety days after demand."

"Yes," Ed Jackson said.

17

"And three months ago the bank sold Kilgore's note to Gideon Markham," Travis said.

"Correct."

"And Gid Markham immediately demanded payment of the note in ninety days," Travis said. "This is the day Kilgore's note is due."

"I'm afraid so," said Ed Jackson regretfully.

Travis said pleasantly, "I rode in ahead of Matt Kilgore to take up his note for him."

Ed Jackson looked startled. Then his pleased smile came. "I'll get it," he said, leaving his chair. He had a satisfied, excited look as he hurried out.

A pleasant sense of power filled Travis as he looked idly at the polished brass cuspidor and the scenic lithographs on the walls. This was what money could do. Buying Kilgore's note was a gamble, although not an unpleasurable one. He was beginning to like Matt Kilgore and Kilgore's daughter Patricia. Travis sat musing on what the Kilgores were going to mean to him.

Ed Jackson was wondering somewhat the same thing as he opened the bank's black metal note box. He was pleased at what was happening and covertly excited, too, because he suspected that fierce emotions and possibly fiercer acts would now be unleashed. Ed was smiling as he walked back to his creaking swivel chair.

Travis stood up and walked to the window with an air of held-in force. The blue broadcloth coat was snug over wide shoulders. Sunlight through the window highlighted auburn tints in his curly hair. And, to his credit, Ed Jackson had noted, Travis ignored the custom of the country and went unarmed.

The look of leashed force was on the rugged, long-boned face which Travis turned from the window. The cool awareness of wide experience was in the alert blue eyes. "You knew when you sold the note to Markham that it would be called on Matt Kilgore."

"When the loan committee voted to take Gid Markham's offer, I went to Kilgore," said Ed Jackson defensively. "Kilgore couldn't offer hope of takin' up his note."

"How much premium did this Markham pay?"

18

"Two thousand dollars," said Ed Jackson uncomfortably.

Travis weighed the statement. "He must have figured Kilgore was ready for the kill."

"Gid Markham," said Ed Jackson slowly, "has waited a long time."

"I'd like to see him when he hears he loses his two-thousand-dollar premium and gets nothing," Travis said, turning back to the window. A moment later he said, "Kilgore is riding into the plaza now. Let's get it over with."

Jackson swung to his desk. "Indians killed two of Matt Kilgore's boys, different times. Dick was his last boy. Losing Dick down there in Central America, on top of his other troubles, just about finished Kilgore. He gave up. Your comin' to Soledad to see about the cattle he bought and was holding for you has done a lot for Matt."

"I almost didn't come. At least for another year or so," Travis said, staring out the window. "Now that I'm here, I seem to be staying on." Travis was smiling as he moved back to his chair.

"I heard," said Ed Jackson, "that a rock slide caught Dick and his horse."

"A one-mule trail in Guatemala, and a drop to a river with rapids and falls," Travis said, sobering. "I was ahead of the *mozo* and pack mules. Dick was riding behind when a sheet of rock let go. He didn't have a chance." Almost believing he had seen it happen, Travis dropped into the chair at the corner of the desk and finished, "Dick was one to go with."

"I always thought so." Ed Jackson looked up. His smile came. "There's Kilgore outside now. Got a whoop back in his voice."

Travis smiled too, faintly, remembering the spiritless greeting that Matt Kilgore had first given him. The man had seemed beaten by bad luck and grief. Boot heels thumping into the bank now had the impact of purpose. And the illusion of size and power which once must have been on Matt Kilgore like a lusty shield filled the office doorway.

Travis got to his feet. Kilgore waved him back. "This ain't no secret."

Matt Kilgore was not a big man, actually. But from worn

19

boot heels past gunbelt, open vest and powerful chest, to the seamed face cut with shadings of fiery force and sadness and lusty humor which reports said the man had once had, Matt Kilgore seemed big. Emotion was in him today, Travis knew, but Matt Kilgore said only, "That note you sold young Markham, Ed, is due. He's in town. Tell 'im the next move is his."

"Roger Travis just bought the note," Ed Jackson said mildly. "Gid Markham's shut out of the matter now."

"Bought it—"

As Matt Kilgore moved forward, Travis had the feeling that the man did not really see him. But a callused, rope-burned hand went out and gripped his arm for an instant as Kilgore walked past the front window. Under his breath, getting it out with difficulty, Matt Kilgore spoke to the dusty window glass. "Seems like Dick come back." Then, not turning, he said, "I passed Patricia outside town with the burro string from her little two-bit mine. She know you done this?"

"No," Travis admitted.

"Well, tell 'er!" Matt Kilgore boomed. "She's ridin' into the plaza now."

Ed Jackson was smiling broadly when Travis walked out and the flat, metallic jangle of burro neck bells was in the plaza.

Patricia Kilgore's long string of pack burros looked diminutive under heavy leather *alforjas* of ore they carried. Two dark-featured Mexicans of the country, father and son, who worked Pat's skimpy little ore vein high on Big Jack Mountain, were walking with the burros. And when Pat Kilgore saw Travis heading to the plaza corner to intercept her, she swung her roan gelding into a run toward him.

Pat sat the sidesaddle like a lithe boy, not even worry subduing her eagerness and zest for life, Travis thought as she came up with a rush, reached down for his hand, and slipped lightly off.

Pat's skirt was rough *manta* cloth of the country, dyed blue. The dried tunnel swipings on her duck jacket showed she had ridden all the way up to the little pack mine which was hers by discovery of the outcrop.

20

"Gid Markham," said Pat rapidly, "is across the plaza with two of his men. Where's Dad?"

"In the bank."

Pat's small strong hand loosened the braided leather *barbiquejo,* the chin strap of her straw sombrero. She pulled off the hat and asked anxiously, "Does he seem to want trouble with Gid today?"

"Didn't seem to," Travis said, holding off mention of the note. He was thinking that Patricia Kilgore reminded him of that dead wife in Wyoming whom he had never seen. She was that vivid girl, unafraid, with eagerness and laughter and a capacity for tenderness.

Pat bit her lip. Her black hair shone darkly in the sun. Her greenish-blue eyes, direct and honest, were clouded now with concern for her father. "Matt's bitter," she said. She would have said more but Travis blocked it.

"Here comes the redhead widow who owns the paper," Travis warned under his breath.

He was stirred again by this Mrs. Strance who published the weekly paper her husband had owned. Lamplight burned late at her desk. Dorothy Strance was everywhere, seeking news, often driving her rattly old buggy out of town, her small daughter usually on the seat with her. She dressed plainly. Dot Strance knew everyone. Her name was never connected with a man. But as she stopped now at the edge of the walk, Travis once more had an uncomfortable awareness of her. She wore a plain cambric wash suit and her flat-brimmed straw hat seemed to sit without thought on the severely pinned, bright hair. But all this could not hide a warm, attractive woman in her restless, eager prime, ripe for affection and wanting it; yet holding back, as if afraid, Travis suspected.

"Mr. Travis, I'm going to print what the *padre* just told me," Dorothy Strance said. Patricia Kilgore's smile turned puzzled, and Dorothy Strance explained, "Mr. Travis just gave the *padre* a hundred dollars, which the *padre* can use, heavens knows. Father Philippe gives everything he has away and lives on beans and chili which he dislikes." An odd intentness suddenly dropped on Dorothy Strance's attractive face as she looked past them.

21

And, when Travis turned and saw the three riders coming across the plaza, he became watchful. Before long, he suspected, he would clash violently with young Gid Markham who led them.

Gid Markham's father had been a shrewd Vermonter who had reached New Mexico with the Mexican War troops in the same company with Matt Kilgore. The elder Markham had married into a leading native family, and the son had a Vermonter's shrewd control laced with hot Mexican pride. The sum of it was a controlled arrogance which made Gid Markham's look toward them now almost like a slap.

Pat Kilgore spoke under her breath. "Gid knows Dad's in the bank. He couldn't wait—" she broke off and caught Travis's arm.

Matt Kilgore's broad-chested figure was sauntering out of the bank with visible expectation. Vest open, thumbs hooked on his wide cartridge belt, Matt's jeer to the three riders pulling up before the bank was audible.

"So the young feller couldn't wait? Greedy like his old man always was. Go in an' pick up your money, boy. I'll be laughin' when you find you're skunked again."

Gid Markham sat in straight, cold silence, curbing his restless horse. Then he wrenched the horse around and drove it toward them. Pat's hand tightened on Travis's arm as Markham pulled up before them. Seen close, he had a wiry, broad-chested look and thin, clean features which showed little of his Mexican heritage. He was wearing sober black; and the hard, bitter anger in his stare at Travis was near violence.

"Kilgore didn't have any money!" he said. "No one but you could've put it up!"

Calmly Travis said, "Well?"

"You came here a stranger and you've butted into things that are none of your business!"

"You wanted your money today. Go in and pick it up," Travis said coolly.

Markham had a belt gun under his open black coat, a carbine in his saddle boot. He wanted to use a gun now. The look was on his thin, cold face. Travis turned his back, and was glad he did when he saw the expression on Mrs. Strance's

22

face as she gazed at the man. . . . There it was in the open, ripe and eager for an unguarded moment, and the resentment Travis felt surprised him.

He heard Markham wheel the horse away. And Pat Kilgore was saying breathlessly, accusingly, with shaken laughter and relief in her tone, "Why didn't you tell me?"

Travis grinned and caught Dorothy Strance's speculative glance. "You do nice things, Mr. Travis," she said. "The *padre*—and now Matt Kilgore." She hesitated. "But you've made an enemy."

"Sorry, ma'am," his smile considered her. "Are you going to print this, too?"

"I'd like to," Dorothy Strance said. "But I'll wait. There might be more to print." The thought seemed to give her no pleasure and Travis suspected why.

4

In early June, in northern Arizona, old Ira Bell watched two strangers approach the yellow sandstone cliffs at the mouth of the canyon called Little Bitter Water by the Navajos.

They rode tired horses and led a pack horse. They were heavily armed, unshaven and rough-looking, but they appeared reasonably honest, Ira Bell decided hopefully as they rode to the wisps of his campfire and dismounted.

He was a leathery little man, dried and brittle as an old sand-scoured cholla cactus. "Howdy," he said. He jerked a thumb at the scattered horse herd nipping sparse bunchgrass back in the narrow canyon. "Ute an' Navvyjo hosses I traded fer." The taller stranger cast a sardonic glance at the horses, and Bell said piously, "Leastways the Utes an' Navs claimed 'em."

The second stranger, a muscular man, broad across heavy

23

cheekbones, said humorously, "If them horses could talk, I bet they'd be cryin', 'Morman settlements.'"

Ira Bell scratched the long gray stubble on his jaw and grinned. "Ain't a hoss said a word. I'm takin' 'em to good feed an' honest ridin' which is all ary man can do. But them two bucks helpin' me is spooked. One seen his mother-in-law's face two weeks ago an' is fixin' to go blind ary day now."

The taller stranger chuckled. "Her face ugly enough to blind him?"

"Ain't that," said Ira Bell tolerantly. "Helps a Navvyjo man get shut of his mother-in-law though. He's chancin' sure blindness to see her face." Bell shook his head. "An' last night a coyote howled at the moon which means bad news. This mornin' when we started, a wildcat run acrost the trail. Means bad luck ahead, so we had to turn back. . . . Goin' blind, bad news comin', bad luck ahead," said Ira Bell, glumly now, "has took them two bucks' stomach fer trailin' down to Soledad in New Mexico. I got to have help."

The tall stranger was reaching for his saddle cinch. "Soledad?" he said, not turning. "Ever hear of a Kilgore family near there?"

"Matt Kilgore," said Ira Bell readily, "owns a big, near-busted ranch he's fixin' to lose before long."

The stranger pulled a straight-stemmed pipe from his shirt pocket. "Ever hear of a man named Travis?"

Hopefully Ira Bell said, "At the Kilgores when I left. You know 'im?"

"Never met him." The bronzed stranger glanced at the yellow cliffs baking in the last red light, and at the sudden alertness of his companion. His smile came and broadened. "I'm Clay Mara. This is Howie Quist. Mother-in-laws don't worry us, or wildcats or coyotes. We'll help to Soledad. Eh, Howie?"

"I was thinkin' so," Howie Quist said.

They were five days from the Little Bitter Water, and the last rank water was forty miles back in the shallow Absalom Well, when the towering pall of a sandstorm advanced like yellow smoke and struck the plodding horse herd.

24

Clay Mara, riding ahead, pulled his red bandanna up over his nose against the first swirling dust. Light faded as the gale settled in and great ground gusts began to drive sand in flat, pelting sheets. Hat yanked low, coat collar turned up, bandanna masking his face to the eyes, Clay shouldered into the belting sand. The wildness of the dry storm stirred memories of what had happened to him, and of what lay ahead.

Even now it was hard to believe that a man he had never seen, whom he would not know when they met, had traveled from Guatemala to San Francisco and had taken his identity and all that he possessed.

Once more Clay recalled the cascading rocks sweeping Dick Kilgore and himself off a narrow trail into the river below. An elderly Indian had fished him out, apparently dead. Cracked ribs, fractured leg, bashed head, had held him helpless in a thatched *jacal*. Dick had never been found. The *mozo* and two pack mules had vanished, into the river also, Clay had decided. When, finally, he had moved on, weak, half-crippled for a time, he had slowly traveled south, and tried to forget.

Only in San Francisco had he realized what must have happened. The *mozo* and pack mules had escaped. A stranger had gotten possession of the mule packs, had found the journal which Roger Travis had kept for years, the certificate of deposit in the South Bay Bank, papers, letters. . . . Now the man was *ahead*.

When Clay looked back, Howie Quist and old Ira Bell were bowed and ghostly figures in the storm. Howie rode forward and shouted ruefully through his masking bandanna, "I bet that bad-luck wildcat them two Navajos seen scratched up this dust!" Then Howie said, "What if we miss them Red Rocks?"

No water beyond the Red Rocks, Ira Bell had said, until the foothills forty-fifty miles on. Too far for the horses. "Stay close to the old man," Clay ordered.

He rode on, peering steadily at the drifted trail. At times he lost it. The wildly buffeting gusts finally lulled a little and vision extended to the warped gray boards of an abandoned wagon bed off to the right. Sand was piling against

25

the boards and streaming over in smokelike veils. . . . And a little beyond, low red rocks were thrusting up from the desert floor. Clay relaxed.

The rocks became a low ridge, a series of higher red ridges, and the trail veered between two crescent ridges into a crude amphitheater where the gale was broken and the flying dust thinned. Howie and Ira Bell rode forward.

Bell's voice was hoarse through his black face cloth. "The tanks is up in them rocks ahead."

Tails, manes blowing, the horses streamed by. Clay followed them to the rocks ahead where the horses were bunching in confused uncertainty, knowing water was close. Clay dismounted and caught the canteen strap off the saddle horn. The muted punch of a gunshot brought him around quickly, as the sound batted off the bald rocks into the gale whining above over the ridges.

Howie and Ira Bell rode close, peering for the source of the shot. A wind-strangled shout drifted down to them. "No water here for them hosses!"

These Red Rock Tanks, Ira Bell had said, were natural catchment basins for the infrequent, furious desert rains. The tanks lay on the ledges of the bald ridge sloping back in front of them. When the lower tanks were dry, water from the higher pools could be thrown down, or carried down— and no man who reached this spot ever minded the labor.

Strong eddies of the gale overhead were sweeping dust across the ridge slope. The man who had shouted was not visible. Clay looked at the horses. Eighty-two had started from the Little Bitter Water, and old Bell's assurance that water would be here at the Red Rocks, in the upper pools, had brought them along without worry.

Tersely, Clay called to the old man, "You said there'd be water!"

Ira Bell's hand gestured helplessly. Tired bewilderment filled his voice. "Was when I come through, headin' north."

Clay turned back to the ridge, shouting at the man he could not see. "What happened to the water?"

"We're holdin' what's left!"

"We're from Absalom Well! These horses can't get through without water!"

26

"Fill canteens if you like!"

Howie yanked the blue bandanna down off his grimy face. "They think they'll make that stick?"

Studying the rocks, Clay said, "Easy, Howie."

The murky sandstorm shrilled across the red rock ridges as Howie Quist swung off his horse in visible outrage. Clay stood beside his restless horse, canteen in hand, trying to stifle the feeling that there was real danger.

This crude amphitheater between two curving arms of the ridges gave a measure of protection from the storm. But a thin dust haze boiled around the milling horse herd. Smoky curtains of dust and sand swept across the higher ledges of the sloping ridge before them. The armed strangers on the upper ledges were invisible. Any water in the tanks up there was being held from Bell's horse herd. . . . But such things were done. The danger Clay could sense was beyond that. It came to him suddenly. The bawled permission to fill canteens was warning enough.

Clay called, "Howie, get Bell's canteen!"

Ira Bell's irritable gesture waved Howie away. "Ain't he'pless! Get m' own water!"

They both watched Bell dismount. The long miles from the Absalom Well had visibly drained the old man. His leathery face had a dried, drawn look of exhaustion under the bristly gray beard stubble as Clay stepped to him and asked, "Any idea who's up there?"

"Passel damn' water hogs! The Absalom Well trail ain't the only one hits by here. Might be anyone."

Clay was looking around. "Where's their camp, their horses?"

"They's another pocket in the rocks half-mile south. . . . Some runty tanks there."

Howie joined them, and Clay said briefly, "They don't mean for us to ride far and tell what happened here."

"Said we could fill canteens," Howie reminded.

"But no water for the horses. Canteen water sounds like bait to draw us up on the rocks, closer." Clay turned to his horse and pulled the carbine from the saddle boot. "I'll take the canteens up alone."

Another wind-muted shout drifted off the ridge slope.

27

"Leave be, you! No raafle ain't needed t' fill canteens!"

Clay's tight smile came as he shoved the carbine back into the boot. "I thought so. Howie, you and Bell move our saddle and pack horses against the edge of the herd."

"I ain't draggin' back while you go up alone!"

"One man might make it. Two'll be a crowd."

"Lemme go then!"

Clay looked up at the opaque clouds of the sandstorm driving overhead. "Be dark before long." His half-smile went to Howie. "First trouble, I'll come rolling and bouncing down."

"I don't like it," said Howie stubbornly.

"Who said I liked it? Get your canteen."

Clay unbuttoned his coat, clearing the holstered gun. Alone, carrying the three empty canteens by their straps, he skirted the slowly milling horse herd and started up the steep slope of the ridge. Great swirls of dust and sand scoured across the higher rocks. Fierce gusts whipped the red kerchief folds under his chin. The violence of the storm was in him again, sweeping gritty, electric over skin nerves.

For a moment Clay wondered if the fellow who was calling himself Roger Travis could be back of this. There had been stories in the San Francisco papers about the abduction of William Campbell from the South Bay Bank by a stranger who had tried to cash a draft against an account in the name of Travis. . . . If the man had read them or had heard of the incident from the bank, he would guess that the real Roger Travis was alive. He would be waiting, watching. This was the only logical trail into Soledad.

A visible way had been worn up the rocks to the tanks which caught the infrequent desert rains. Clay reached the first large, shallow basin which held only sandy muck on the bottom. He climbed on, squinting into the sand and dust blowing across the face of the ridge.

The next tank, not as large, was partially sheltered by an overhang of rock. Yellow dust covered the water. When Clay dropped a canteen in by its strap, the canteen went completely under. Without expression, Clay watched silvery bubbles burst to the surface. He hauled the canteen out and drank deliberately. And when he lowered the canteen, he sighted the first stranger standing on a ledge some thirty feet higher and twice that far off to the right.

Blocky, muscular-looking, hat yanked low, bandanna masking the face against the storm, rifle held ready, the watching figure was a silent threat.

Then on the same ledge, hunkered down, Clay saw the head, shoulders, and rifle of another man watching him. And several more of them must be around in the rocks.

Clay shouted at the silent figure. "Our saddle horses won't make it without water!"

"Fill them canteens an' move out!"

In simmering anger, Clay eyed the man. He remembered how the fellow had said *raafle*. Somewhere he would hear that flat nasal word again and would know this man.

Down below Howie and Ira Bell had brought the saddle horses to the edge of the half-frantic, thirsty herd. A pinto horse broke out of the herd toward the water he could smell. In awkward lunges, hoofs slipping on the smooth rocks, the pinto started to climb. And Clay ducked as a rifle report slapped through the shrilling wind.

When he looked down again, the pinto's brown and white splotches were dropping on the rocks. The blocky stranger on a higher ledge was unconcernedly jacking in another shell.

Ira Bell's shrill anger drifted up. "That hoss belonged to Gid Markham!"

The stranger in the rocks above Clay shouted down at Ira Bell in a startled tone, "What's a Markham hoss doin' in your bunch?"

"I been buyin' hosses fer Gid Markham," Ira Bell said. "He'll hunt you down! He won't never stop!"

Clay could have groaned as he heard the exchange and jerked the filled canteens out of the water. Old Ira Bell's rage had done it now. They'd not get to this Gid Markham —whoever he was—if they could be stopped.

Clay was swiftly stoppering the dripping canteens when the shot he expected breached through the storm. . . . And the sound had its mockery for his own plans. If this were the end, the man named Roger Travis had his freedom to enjoy the identity, the money he had stolen.

29

The heavy canteens banged against Clay's legs as he lunged up. Howie and Ira Bell were dodging behind the saddle horses, and beyond Bell one of the herd horses was dropping.

5

That first bullet, Clay saw, had been meant for Ira Bell. Clay jumped recklessly down the steep slope, guessing that he was the next target. The heavy canteens, two in one hand, the tilted ledges and smooth rock falling away through swirling dust, made it an awesome, dangerous descent for a running man.

In the first plunging steps, gravity and the treacherous footing took over. Every jarring stride risked disaster. Other guns on the upper ledges were firing now. A bullet missed Clay's shoulder. He heard the thin lash of its passing.

Below, in blurred glimpses, he saw Howie Quist and old man Bell driving shots from their saddle guns at the ledges. His right foot skidded on smooth rock. A desperate lunge and twist staved off the fall and threw him down the steep slope faster, faster. A blow on the canteens vibrated up through the straps.

A foot skidded. Clay reeled over a narrow ledge and leaped at the next drop. Arms frantically windmilling with the canteens, he raced down the last steep slope and hurtled on into the milling horse herd.

He struck the side of a stocky roan, driving the horse staggering. And careened off against another horse which whinnied and reared. Bouncing off the twisting animal, Clay skidded along the flank of another and came to a gasping, sliding halt in the midst of the alarmed herd.

He was gripping the canteen straps so tightly his fists ached. Water was spurting against his right leg. The two canteens in that hand had been drilled by a bullet and were emptying fast. Clay bolted on, shouting a way through the herd.

Ira Bell and Howie were firing across their saddles when Clay tossed canteen loops over his own saddle horn and gasped, "Lead your horses out until the dust gives cover!"

And as they ran, crouching, leading the saddle horses through the alarmed scattering of the herd, what Clay feared might happen, did happen. Howie Quist's horse was driven to its knees by a bullet. Howie swung around, studied the ridges and fired.

Dust thickened behind them as they ran on. Ira Bell was stumbling and gasping for breath when Clay swerved to him and called, "Get in the saddle!"

Bell reached to the saddle horn and sagged there against the horse. Clay's rough boost shoved the small, shuddering figure up. A yell, a blow of his fist started the horse sluggishly out toward the full, fierce sweep of the sandstorm.

A screen of scattering herd horses followed as Howie ran with Clay another hundred yards. Howie had no horse now. Clay finally ordered, "Climb on my horse! I'll straddle behind you!"

Riding that way, they passed out of the trapping amphitheater. Ira Bell had pulled his horse up and sat in an exhausted slump, hat askew, eyes dull in the dusty sockets of his leathery face.

The old man, Clay saw, would be useless in any more fighting. He might collapse suddenly and they would have him on their hands. Clay slid off, caught the one full canteen from the saddle horn and gave it to the old man. And to Howie, Clay called, "Ought to be some water in those two holed canteens. Get it in you!" He wheeled back, watching for pursuit while the two men drank greedily.

Bell's gnarled hands were shaking when he lowered the canteen strap to the saddle horn. Clay shouldered through the blowing sand to the bowed, gnomelike figure and asked, "Can you make the hills on that one canteen?"

Bell's voice had a drained thinness. "Might. This hoss can't."

"After your talk of Gid Markham, they'll be after us,"

31

Clay guessed with harsh conviction. "Howie and I have got to find their horses and more water. If you give out, you'll burden us too much. Ride for Soledad now, old man. With luck, you might make it."

"I won't burden you," Ira Bell said. His shaking hand pulled the black kerchief up over his bristle of gray face stubble. Slowly he lifted the reins and urged the horse into a tired walk. Shoulders bowed, the old man rode from sight into the driving sheets of sand.

Howie Quist gazed after him and shook his head. "The old fellow might make it," Howie said. He turned a canteen upside down and watched the last drops whirled away by the wind. "Most a pint was left; pure honey," Howie said gratefully. He held out the second canteen.

"I got mine up at the tank," Clay said. He straddled behind Howie again, holding his carbine. "South along the ridge," he ordered. "They'll be running to their camp for horses."

Over a shoulder, Howie said, "Suppose there ain't a camp?"

"They didn't walk here. Has to be a camp."

Howie changed the subject. "Thought the old fellow was tradin' with the Navajos on his own hook. Who's this Markham?"

"Never heard of him," Clay said. He was bracing with a palm against Howie's side, and was conscious, suddenly of a damp splotch on Howie's coat. "What's wrong, Howie?" Clay asked evenly.

"Cracked rib maybe," said Howie carelessly.

Clay's exploring fingers found the little ragged bullet hole in the coat cloth. Quietly he asked, "How bad, Howie?"

"It didn't come near the lung, I reckon," Howie said casually. "Nothin' risin' in my throat. I'm good for all night."

Howie was wrong. They both knew it. Howie was losing blood, losing strength, in a hot gale relentlessly drying him out. Howie would fade fast now unless he had water and a tight bandage over the wound. Ruthlessly Clay spurred the horse which already had done too much today.

Tumbleweeds whisked past like erratic, bouncing ghosts lost in the storm. The spurred, straining horse skirted long

32

wind-wrenched stalks of *ocotillo* cactus, called Mexican Wife-Beaters. . . . And the sand-drifted talus at the foot of the almost vertical ridge they were following gave way to dust-filled space.

"Got to be it," Clay decided. "Take guard here. I'll handle what's inside!"

He slid off, shoved the carbine into Howie's hand and ran forward, not looking back. And once more the high, bald ridges blotted the full drive of the wind. Clay ran through swirling, finer dust, his boots grinding on sand laid down by other storms.

The camp, suddenly, was there in front of him, to the right where the ridge bent back. He saw picketed horses first. Nine horses looming in the veiling dust on ropes and pins. On the ground beyond was a litter of saddles, bridles, blanket rolls, and the black, drifted circle of a small cook fire.

It was the meager, hasty camp of men who had come riding light and meant to leave that way. Clay counted the saddles as he neared them. Seven saddles. He began to believe as he came in at a slogging run that no guard had been left. It was almost his undoing.

Hunkered motionless in a cleft of the ridge rock, the guard had pulled a blanket over his head. The crouched figure resembled a hummock of blown sand. From the corner of an eye Clay barely caught the slight motion of the blanket being lifted. A bandanna, red like the cloth over Clay's face, masked the guard's face against the wind. His call, sharply inquiring but not fully alarmed, cut through the boisterous turbulence of the gust.

"That you, Slim?"

"Yes!" Clay answered and swerved toward the rock.

The hunkered figure was struggling up, wiry and lean, canvas jacket buttoned over shell belt and holster.

Clay was strides away, still picking up momentum, when he saw the stiffening instant of doubt as the guard peered hard at him. A hand caught for a carbine leaning against the rock, and Clay reached under his coat.

The guard was hemmed against the rock, frantically jacking in a shell as Clay reached him and slapped the carbine

33

muzzle aside. The guard ducked. Clay slammed his hand-gun across the black hat brim and his full running weight smashed into the man.

They hurtled together against the rock. They fell together, Clay on top. The guard struggled desperately. Clay thought of the thirsty paint horse callously shot. He struck again with the heavy gun barrel. The struggling figure went loose and quiet and Clay shoved upright.

Gasping, he tore the red bandanna off the guard's face and printed the pinched, slack features in memory. He yanked a cedar-handled revolver from the holster under the man's canvas jacket and ran to the sand-drifted saddles and caught up a gaudy saddle blanket of Navajo weave, a bridle and a saddle.

The powerful blood bay he selected took the bit, blanket and saddle without protest. Clay reached back for his knife in its leather hip sheath. Deliberately he went among the saddles, ruthlessly slashing stirrup and cinch straps. He jerked a blanket roll open and piled a tangle of bridles and reins on the blanket and knotted them in.

Canteens lay among the saddles. Clay hung them in a heavy clutter on his saddle horn. Explosive breaths were pushing out the red cloth over his face as he caught up the guard's carbine and smashed the stock against the earth. The guard was huddled motionless in the rock cleft when Clay gave him a last look and began to cut the picket ropes.

It took moments of dragging and hauling to get the horses lined around and all lead ropes in one hand. Clay heard the wind-muted punch of gunfire as he heaved the blanket bundle to the bay's neck. He topped the saddle with an up-ward lunge, balanced the bundle in his lap, and slowly reined the blood bay away.

The lead horses came around and moved with him. Slowly Clay stepped up the pace, riding faster, faster through the swirling veils of dust.

The horses were massed and running when they burst out into the full thrashing force of the storm. Clay glimpsed Howie Quist off to the right, spurring his jaded horse at a tangent. Gunshots were faint off to the left as Clay led the trampling rush of horses into the veiling maw of the sand-storm.

Howie rode alongside. "Gimme some of them ropes!" he yelled and caught them in a big hand. His question cracked through the blue face cloth. "You clean out their camp?"

"Tried to." Clay waved Howie on. They had ridden out from the ridges for miles before Clay pulled up and said, "I'll get your saddle on a fresh horse. Water in those canteens."

Howie dismounted with slow effort. His voice had a new exhausted note. "Two come in on foot. The rest was followin', I think."

"I cut their cinches and stirrup straps and put 'em afoot without bridles or water," Clay said grimly. "But they'll water some of Bell's horses, rig hackamores and come on bareback."

Keeping his back to the wind and sand when possible, Clay transferred the saddle to a short-coupled roan with powerful withers and the look of bottom. He dumped the mass of bridles and reins out of the blanket and reached for his sheath knife to slash strips off the blanket.

"Open up that side, Howie. Got a corset for you."

They stood in the lee of the massed horses and Howie Quist opened his coat and shirt. There was no time for swabbing or probing. Only time in short, sand-lashed minutes to shove the rough blanket strips around Howie's powerful back and haul the strips tight until the torn, gaping wound was bound in. Clay tied the strips with hard knots.

"Ought to do you," he said finally.

Howie drew a constricted breath as he closed his shirt and grinned wanly. "If this is how a corset feels," said Howie, "I'd rather bleed."

There was one last chore. Clay used the keen sheath knife on the tangle of bridles and reins. The short lengths he hurled aside would never help guide a horse.

They rode again and night seeped in, filled with the shrill of the wind and rattling assault of blown debris. And they were both conscious that old Ira Bell, bowed, silent, alone on a ridden-out horse, was also moving through the blackness. If his horse had lasted this long.

35

A long time later Howie called, "Ain't it easin' a little?"

Milder notes were in the violence of the gale. In another half-hour the disk of the moon could be located. The wind continued to die. In the quiet that fell, the scuffing steps of the horses had an unreal loudness.

"They know we're heading this way," Clay said.

"Big country . . . no tracks," Howie said. He sounded drowsy. Clay saw that Howie was sagging as he rode.

"Howie! Drink more water," Clay said, loudly. He had to repeat it before Howie's hand slowly went to a canteen.

"Like t' catch some sleep," Howie muttered.

A man began to die like this in the desert. Dried-out, bled-out, he slowly faded like Howie was fading.

Clay rode close and said, "Hold up, Howie!" He dropped the lead ropes, leaned far out and shoved a hand under the dusty coat which Howie had unbuttoned when the wind had died. The blanket strips had a foreboding stiffness. "Wait!" Clay said. He swung down, stripped headstalls and ropes off all the lead horses but one and slapped them away. "They'll head for the hills and leave fresh tracks to puzzle over," Clay said. And when he looked again at Howie, Clay said roughly, "Keep awake!"

"Sure," agreed Howie docilely.

Clay's mouth was a hard line when he topped the saddle again, holding the single lead rope of the extra horse. "Going to cut north a little," Clay said. "Old man Bell should be over that way if he kept going."

"Ol' coot's tough," Howie said. The drowsy note was stronger, warning of what was happening.

It was sometime after midnight. Howie had a good chance if they headed straight for the hills. But moonlight on the desert floor was bright enough to sight fresh tracks. Clay made the reluctant decision. Howie, riding sleepily and agreeably, made no protest as they angled off the direct line to the hills and safety, and rode to find old Ira Bell, if possible.

6

Eastward some seventy miles, the gray dawn brightened along the horizon and sunrise came. And, a little later, Patricia Kilgore went motionless before the marble top of her bedroom dresser, with three hairpins forgotten in the corner of her smiling mouth.

Matt Kilgore's off-key singing had not boomed like this in years. In the wide yard behind the house, sawing, hammering, men's voices were audible. Listlessness and defeat had vanished on the ranch. It was stimulating, exciting—and Roger Travis had brought it all about.

Each day now Patricia's gratitude increased. This morning Roger was riding into Soledad, and she was riding part way with him. When Patricia walked out of the house, carrying her straw sombrero by its braided leather chin ties, her roan gelding and Roger's horse were saddled and waiting in the yard.

Roger and her father were talking beside the horses. The old look of force and lusty humor was on Matt as he balanced on worn boot heels, sunlight in his shock of graying hair, one hand chopping gestures. Roger had his reassuring look of bigness and assurance as both men smiled indulgently at her.

"Your father," Roger said lightly, "wants me to wear a gun." He gave her a hand up to the sidesaddle and smiled up at her. "And all I want is friends."

Matt was blunt. "In town the other day, Gid Markham put you in his tally book, son. Gid don't forget."

A faint tightness touched Patricia's throat. Once more Matt could say, "Son," unconsciously, and feel it when he talked to Roger Travis.

As their horses wheeled away, Patricia looked about the busy yard. Beyond the half-finished bunkhouse, native

Mexicans were molding adobe bricks from puddled mud and straw. A freight wagon which had rolled in during a high windstorm last night was being unloaded.

Roger Travis grinned at her. "Be a different ranch when we're through. Big plans ahead."

"What plans?" Patricia countered pointedly.

He stared into distance, riding with the straight assurance that was so much a part of him. "It's a big country. A man can grow big in it if he plans right."

"And if he has enough money," said Patricia lightly.

"I've got money." For a moment Roger Travis seemed alone with his thoughts as he looked across the miles of undulating grass to blue mountains against the cloudless sky.

All her life Patricia had known this rugged land, often harsh and always beautiful. She had for an instant now the exciting sensation of viewing it in new promise through the eyes of Roger Travis.

He said, "All my life I've been looking for something like this." His smile sought her. "Even the pretty girls own mines."

Patricia chuckled. "Last year my mine cleared about three hundred dollars. But I found the outcrop; it's something that I own myself."

Roger changed the subject. "What started all this trouble with the Markhams?"

"Amos Markham, Gid's father, started it. Not even Dad knows why."

"I've heard they were friends in the Army during the Mexican War."

"They enlisted in St. Louis on the same day. They were discharged together and were friends until after Amos married the daughter of old Lorenzo Rivera."

"Sometimes a woman—"

"Wrong guess," Patricia said, smiling. "Dad met Mother during a trip to Santa Fe. They were married in a week. Amos had never seen Mother until he married Consuela Rivera shortly after."

"Something started the trouble."

"When Dad started his own ranch there was trouble

38

from the first," Patricia said, trying to keep bitterness out of her tone. "Amos was shrewd. He added to the Rivera holdings. But he became cold and hard. Matt jeered at the change in him and fought him through the years. . . . Until the boys were gone. Now Gid Markham is carrying it on."

"We'll take care of Gid Markham," Roger said. He was smiling again when Patricia looked at him. He stayed warmly in her mind after she turned off alone, riding a faint trail through the lifting, pine-dotted foothills.

The trail from her small pack mine dropped off Big Jack Mountain through a precipitous little canyon. A narrow stream widened over stony shallows as it broke out of the mouth of the canyon. The trail on the stream bank held fresh sign this morning which said that the long string of pack burros loaded with ore had already passed this point on the way to Soledad. Patricia shook her horse into a lope, and some miles beyond she sighted an approaching rider. She couldn't believe it. Never had she known Gid Markham's mother to appear like this on land controlled by the Kilgores.

The woman had been a mystery most of Patricia's life, little more than a shadowy name from which the fierce, unhappy past had sprung. Since her husband had died, Consuela Markham had been away much of the time, traveling widely, Patricia knew from reading the weekly *Soledad Beacon*.

This woman was not from the little native *placitas*, with her head covered by a black *rebozo*, Patricia saw as they neared each other. The black serge riding habit, black gloves of soft leather, small black hat would match any in the Territory.

Consuela Markham curbed her spirited dun horse and spoke first. "Your burro man said you might come this way." She had hardly an accent. Her small-boned face held pride which had been given to Gid Markham. Level brown eyes were direct and curious. "Like your mother," the woman said.

She didn't like my mother, Patricia sensed. She made no comment as the woman reined her horse back and they rode on together.

39

Consuela Markham said, "I have been away this year. Now I hear that a man named Travis is at your ranch. Many things are happening. Plans are being made."

"One plan didn't work when your son bought our note at the bank," said Patricia calmly.

"Gideon is what my husband made him," Consuela Markham said; but when she added, "Amos Markham is dead; Gideon is *my* son now." Patricia looked quickly at her. The soft fierceness and sadness in the woman's words were startling. "There must not be trouble again between the men we have left."

"Why should there ever have been trouble?" Patricia countered.

"It is ended now." The woman's face, hardly lined, and showing a measure of beauty she once must have had as a young girl, looked pale against the black hat and riding habit. "Last night," Consuela Markham said slowly, "Gideon put his hand upon the Bible and promised peace with your family, if not provoked. But this man Travis— What will he do?"

"Why should he do anything?" Patricia said. "Roger is like one of the family now. He wants friends."

"One of the family," said Consuela Markham under her breath. "Another son." Her black-gloved hand made a gesture of finality. "Gideon promised. It must not happen." She wheeled off the trail. The dun's skimming run descended the long slope, weaving among gnarled piñons and cedars, and passed from sight.

She rides better than I do. . . Gid is her son now. . . What did she possess while Amos Markham was alive?

Disturbed by the meeting, Patricia put her roan into a fast lope. And when she turned into the pounded ruts of the Soledad road, she sighted presently the string of pack burros halted ahead under the heavy leather *alforjas* of selected ore. José Sanchez and his grown son who worked the little mine in shares must have started long before dawn. A dusty two-horse buggy halted in the road by the burros made Patricia smile. Dorothy Strance talked with everyone, even José Sanchez, seeking news for her paper. Dot Strance was standing beside the buggy now, binoculars to her eyes, looking west.

The widow lowered the glasses when Pat rode up. She sounded uncertain. "A man is walking in the wash out there, leading a horse and trying to keep from sight, I think."

"An Indian?" Patricia asked quickly.

"No," Dot Strance said, "but he's carrying a rifle ready to use. It looks like two bodies are on the horse he's leading. He could be dangerous."

7

Since sunrise Clay Mara had been dangerous in the way of a man who meant to survive. Last night in moonlight he had finally found fresh boot tracks, and had followed the erratic trail to old Ira Bell, sprawled flat, horse collapsed far back somewhere, water and hope run out.

Bell stayed on the bare back of the spare sorrel horse where Clay had boosted him. And, in the first gray dawn, a shot had reached at them from the black rocks of an ancient lava dike off to the right. Howie Quist's horse had dropped.

Clay had wrenched the big blood bay under him directly at the lava. One man riding far and fast from the Red Rock Tanks had found them and had tried to stop them. He was back there in the silent distance, near the horse on which he had tried to escape. But, before he had flushed into flight, he had crippled the blood bay.

Only the blaze-faced sorrel under Ira Bell had been left. That horse, taken from the camp at the Red Rocks, had had to carry Howie Quist also. Clay had walked.

Since sunrise the green mountains had loomed ahead, tantalizing a man on foot. Hour by slogging hour Clay had

41

walked toward the foothills, and finally up the dry channel of a wash. His boots crunched softly on the loose sand and gravel. Feet had swelled, blisters had lifted and burst. A man this weary was one sodden ache. The lead rope back to the horse ran over Clay's left shoulder. He leaned tiredly forward against the rope when the sorrel dragged back.

Howie Quist lay forward on the bareback horse, eyes closed, hands clutching chunks of rough mane. Ira Bell sagged forward against Howie's back. The sun laid shimmering dazzle and heat in the dry channel. Clay's eyelids felt abraded and raw inside from the sandstorm as he squinted at grass clumps on the banks, at cactus and brush which offered cover for a gun.

When he heard the earth-muffled run of a horse, Clay dropped the rope, shook his head to clear it, and jacked a shell into the carbine. The bank of the wash was above his head along here. The crown of a straw sombrero raking across the background of blue sky was the first thing he sighted. Clay lined the carbine sights swiftly as the rider burst into full view and pulled up on the bank edge.

In the brilliant light, her long blue skirt swept down from the sidesaddle. She was young like Vicky, buried back in Wyoming. She had black hair like Vicky. Clay closed his eyes against the shimmering light which could play such tricks. And her strained voice reached at him. "Do you shoot women?"

"Not today," Clay said hoarsely as he lowered the carbine and opened his eyes.

She reined the horse half around and beckoned. Clay was instantly suspicious. "Who you signaling?"

"A buggy that seems to be needed here." She poised on the sidesaddle slim and lithe as a boy, looking down at him with alert judgment. Her cooling voice demanded, "What are you afraid of?"

"Just careful," Clay said, harshly again because his throat brought it out that way.

"Wait there," she said, wheeled the roan horse and was gone.

Ira Bell slowly pushed himself up off Howie's back and mumbled, "Heerd somethin' like a woman."

42

Clay wiped a coat sleeve over his forehead. Memory of the slim, cool figure judging him suspiciously from the bank edge loosed a bit of garrulous nonsense back at Bell. "Another wildcat crossed our path and we can't turn back," Clay said, grinning stiffly.

Ira Bell slid off, staggered, and braced against the horse's rump. Howie Quist lay limply forward on the sorrel's neck, eyes closed, hands locked in the mane.

Moments later Clay sighted the black buggy top. Paced by the girl on the roan horse, the buggy careened down into the wash. Steel-tired wheels clashed over gravel and small rocks toward them.

Ira Bell, still braced against the horse with an unsteady hand, peered toward the buggy. His voice was a weak croak. "Widder Strance drivin'. That 'n on the hoss is the Kilgore gal."

"Matt Kilgore's daughter?" Clay blurted.

"Uh-huh."

In the dulled corridors of Clay's mind, danger gathered. Today he could not face Travis.

"Old man," Clay reminded harshly, "last night I hunted for you. I brought you this far! You owe me!" Ira Bell's cloudy eyes stared at him from dusty, red-rimmed sockets, and Clay continued urgently. "Forget anything I ever said about this part of the country! When we came by your horse camp that first day, Howie and I were riding for Santa Fe. You hired us. Nothing else was said! Understand?"

Ira Bell's weak nod was uncertain.

Clay surveyed the old man without much hope. Bell's exhausted mind would probably ramble and say that this Clay Mara had inquired about the Kilgore ranch, about the man named Travis. *That would do it if Travis heard.*

Danger brought strength as Clay turned warily and watched this sister of Dick Kilgore ride to him. Dick had called her Pat in the fond way of an older brother. Her hand braced lightly on his callused palm and she dropped off the sidesaddle with a boy's litheness.

Greenish blue eyes gave Clay a direct look and reached past him. "Mr. Bell! I didn't recognize you! What happened?"

Ira Bell's exhausted, gnomelike figure braced against the horse while his mouth opened in the bristle of gray beard stubble and then slowly closed.

"Had a little trouble," Clay said.

Pat Kilgore looked at his gaunt, dust-grimed figure with open suspicion now. "That's plain enough, isn't it? What sort of trouble?"

"Sandstorm for one thing. Anyone could guess." It came out harsh and curt from his raw throat to shut off her questions, and Pat Kilgore reddened as she turned away to meet the arriving buggy.

The two men who clambered quickly out were roughly dressed natives of the country, their dark-brown faces broad in the cheekbones from admixture of Indian blood. Candle drippings on patched denim jackets and worn brogan shoes suggested they were hard-rock miners.

And the woman leaving the buggy on the other side would be the Widow Strance. Clay squinted at her plain cotton wash suit and flat-brimmed straw hat pinned on red hair pulled severely back. He was not too exhausted to have the wry thought that this young widow deserved clothes less plain.

If the woman guessed his thought, she gave no sign. Her question was businesslike. "What's wrong with that one on the horse?"

"Bullet wound. Old Bell's played out."

Her glance dropped to the carbine in his hand. Her order to the older Mexican was brisk. "Sanchez, you and your son put that one on the horse into the buggy. Patricia, you hold the team while they're loading him in."

The grimy corners of Clay's mouth moved in humor. This widow talked briskly, competently; but she didn't look that way at all beneath her severely pinned hair and plain dress. She looked young, warm, friendly. Taller than Pat Kilgore, she stepped beside Clay as he put a hand to Howie Quist's shoulder.

"Howie!" Clay said sharply.

Howie merely muttered as he lay forward on the horse's neck, fists still full of mane. Clay's cuff knocked Howie's head sagging over. The widow Strance drew breath audibly.

44

Behind them Pat Kilgore's indignant protest came. "Do you have to abuse a helpless man?"

Brown hair was a tangled, gritty shock above Howie's broad, unshaven, dusty face as it rolled back into the horse's mane and slowly lifted. Gray-faced with weakness, Howie gazed at the woman beside Clay. Howie's face contorted in the ghost of a dazed grin.

"Out here'n a dry wash—redheaded an' purty!"

"He'll do," said Clay with relief. "Load him in." He had been afraid that Howie was slipping away past help, and had shocked Howie alive with a brutal cuff to the face. Now Howie would make it.

Pat Kilgore, holding the bits of the buggy horses, looked at Clay with angry aversion while the two Mexicans took charge of Howie. Clay eyed her curiously. Made a man feel queer knowing a vivid, pretty girl like this was friendly with a stranger who was using his own identity.

"Do you have to stare?" she demanded shortly.

Clay's brief grin considered her. "Worth it," he said, and when her oval face flushed he turned, satisfied, to the two Mexicans getting Howie's muscular bulk into the buggy. The Widow Strance was supervising. Amusement had glinted in her eyes at Howie's dazed amazement. Clay told her, "I'd like to see Howie to the doctor."

"I'll need you anyway to watch him," Mrs. Strance said briskly. "Get in."

"And I want this horse brought in."

"Sanchez will bring him in."

Ira Bell was helped in, and had to hunch on the floor of the buggy. Even with that, Mrs. Strance was crowded close against Clay as she drove the buggy slowly out of the wash. Without turning her head, she asked, "Do you want to tell me what happened?"

"Not now."

"Your name then?"

"Clay Mara."

The lurching buggy threw them together. "I own the newspaper in Soledad," she said calmly. "And I usually learn everything that happens in this part of the Territory and print it."

45

Clay's chuckle had a flat hardness short of humor as he realized how dangerous this woman could be to his plans. "I'll read it in your newspaper then, ma'am."

Another lurch threw them together again. Her body had a pliant, lithe feel against him. Her cheek was a smooth, soft sweep. Subdued fire lurked in her hair under the plain straw hat. And, as they rode pressed closely together, the glint in the Widow Strance's hazel eyes was a challenge.

"You *will* read it in my paper, Mr. Mara. Who you are, and why you've come in on foot with a wounded man."

Clay was fighting the sleep of complete exhaustion now as the comfortable buggy seat rocked him. He wondered what the Widow Strance would do if his head sagged over on her shoulder.

"I've got to talk to Gid Markham," Clay remembered. "You know him?"

He felt the quick tension of her slim figure. Her question sharpened. "What does Gid have to do with this?"

Clay fought an overpowering yawn, and a growing sense of the warm figure pressed closely against him. "Might be he'll tell you, ma'am. Get word to him anyway."

"Gid," she said after a moment, "may be in town. If not, I'll see that he hears."

This competent, warm, pretty young widow was even more of a threat to his plans than Patricia Kilgore, Clay was realizing. She probably knew Travis. She certainly would try to make old Ira Bell talk. The widow's shoulder close against him drew his thoughts in drowsy fascination. It would be a soft, comfortable shoulder to doze on, Clay caught himself thinking. After a time, he knew he was going to try it.

8

After Pat Kilgore had left him, Roger Travis had turned off the ranch road also. Pressing his horse through winding draws where yellow-topped rabbit weed and orchid flowers of skunkweed dotted color across the grama grass, Travis had thought once more that to the farthest horizons this was a fair country waiting for the bold man who could stand astride it.

His blowing horse finally quartered down a brushy slope and swung up a wide draw. Presently, a quarter-mile ahead, a small slab-rock cabin and cedar-pole corral huddled against a low limestone cliff. This was the outer line camp on the Kilgore ranch, nearest Soledad.

A man stepped on a horse and ran down the draw to meet Travis. He was slender, wiry in sun-faded jeans and gray shirt. His features had the tanned smoothness of youth set now in urgency as he swung the horse around, walking beside Travis. "You see any strangers, Mr. Travis?"

Travis alerted. "Were you followed, Chet?"

"Near run into Gid Markham's mother ridin' this way." Chet's clear eyes under the yanked-down brim of his black hat were worried. "Maybe Markham's ridin' this way, too. He wouldn't take drawin' his pay an' meetin' you like this."

Travis chuckled. "He'd fire you, Chet—and you'd pick up your extra pay from me, go to work for Matt Kilgore and laugh about it."

"Gid Markham," said Chet levelly, "might not figure it that easy."

Travis lost his humor. "Markham thinks he's a Spanish don running an old-time hacienda with peons he can use a whip on!"

"He's proud," Chet said.

47

"He's hard and cold like his old man was. Keep that in mind, Chet." Travis weighed the worry on Chet's face. It was an honest, plain kind of face with its own youthful strength, which was why he was using Chet Davis. "Ever know a finer man than Matt Kilgore, Chet?" Travis asked quietly.

"Never did," said Chet with quick, warming emphasis. "I mind one time when Pa—"

"Matt Kilgore needs help," Travis said gravely. "His boys are gone. The Markhams never have let up on him. You're helping Matt now, Chet. I'm helping him. You're not going to back out?"

"I reckon not," Chet said uncomfortably.

"Matt will be grateful. Now then—is Gid Markham hiring more men? Making moves like trouble?"

"Don't seem so."

"See you here next week then." Travis looked ahead at the small rock cabin and empty corral. "Where's Grady Doyle and his men?"

"They ain't here. An' good riddance if they ain't never back," Chet Davis said coolly. "Ary one would lief shoot a man's back."

Thoughtfully Travis watched Chet Davis ride back down the draw. Too young, too honest. Only Matt Kilgore's name would hold him.

Travis glanced inside the rock hut and stepped back on the horse with growing irritation. He had no illusions about Grady Doyle and the scum Doyle knew how to hire. They'd be back; their pay was too good. But their orders had been to stay here at the line camp.

Riding up the steep head of the draw into scrub cedars, Travis fell to whistling softly as he thought of Patricia Kilgore. Today Pat and he would eat in Soledad. They would ride back to the ranch together. . . . He was still thinking of Pat and the future when the last balding ridges dropped away to the stage road, and Soledad was near. Not much of a town by cities Travis had known. Mostly adobe in the custom of this dry, southwestern land. Little silver-threading irrigation *acequias* ran to green garden plots and tall cottonwoods and elms.

Beyond the brief foothills desert and near-desert ran into distance. But east and south of Soledad the blue peaks lifted. Between them and beyond were deep canyons, rugged hills, great sweeps of grassland, sheltered valleys and more mountains.

This colorful, wild New Mexico country was larger than many Eastern states. Tiny settlements of the native Mexican people had drowsed away the generations. Land, cattle, mines and timber were here. And Travis had quickly realized that a clever stranger with money and luck could dominate all this country. Cattle already branded in his name were here. The Kilgore's run-down ranch was a start.

Soledad was the key. Mines back in the mountains, ranches, little native *placitas* over immense reaches looked to this isolated town. The sheriff and courthouse were a hundred and fifty miles east and south, out of the way.

Travis was smiling when he rode into the busy plaza and stopped at the bank to deposit twenty thousand dollars' worth of St. Louis Exchange. With amusement he knew that the graying Ed Jackson who ran the bank was speculating on how much more money Roger Travis could deposit. Other men, too, were wondering.

At Ledfesser's Mercantile, Travis left a list to be made up. Then, in the Bonanza Bar across the plaza, he bought for the house. Later, Travis would remember this hour in Soledad as the high point of his life. He was happy, lucky, and the future beckoned. The back mirror showed his wide shoulders relaxed in the expensive blue broadcloth suit. His hat was cocked slightly. Travis was laughing when a man touched his elbow and said, "Matt Kilgore's girl wants you outside."

That was the high point, Travis remembered later— Patricia Kilgore waiting outside for him.

Patricia stood a respectable distance from the Bonanza, thinking in anger of the man named Clay Mara. When Roger came to her, tall and smiling, Patricia asked rapidly, "Did you see Dot Strance bring three men into town in her buggy?"

Roger was amused. "Is the widow collecting men today?"

49

"One of the men," said Patricia, "is helpless from a bullet wound. Old Ira Bell is in bad shape. And the horse-thief named Clay Mara who brought them in on one of our horses was so exhausted he slept on Dot's shoulder. They're at Doctor Halvord's house. This man Mara can be caught there."

"One of our horses?" Roger asked quickly. He used "our" like one of the family now. Patricia had seen Matt's pleased smile at hearing it.

"Matt," she reminded, "doesn't like to mark a horse. He brands on the neck where the mane hides it. This sorrel has our brand. Also," said Patricia, with growing heat as she thought of the stranger who had stolen the sorrel, "I remember the three-cornered blaze and white stocking. That horse was in the extra bunch at Canyon Largo."

Little points of cold light jumped into Roger's eyes. Tension edged his words. "That sorrel and two more horses, Pat, were turned over to some men that I—that Matt hired. They went off on business of their own. I don't know what."

Patricia felt let down as she and Roger walked slowly toward the plaza corner. The real worry that had made her seek Roger for advice was only partially lessened by his explanation about the horse.

"This man Clay Mara," she continued under her breath, "asked Dot Strance to send word quickly to Gid Markham."

"Why Markham?" Roger demanded sharply.

"Dot doesn't know. She's afraid it may mean trouble of some sort."

"Does Mrs. Strance know we own the sorrel?"

"I'm sure she doesn't," Patricia said, thinking back. "The neck brand was hidden when Dot stood by the horse. But this man Mara knew who I was, and he didn't mention the sorrel. He was in the buggy with Dot, where I couldn't hear, when he asked her to send for Gid Markham. And he made a point of asking Dot to have the sorrel brought into town, as if he had a reason."

Roger's jaw muscles were bunching. Temper hardened his words. "A wounded man means a gunfight. Matt's men had the sorrel, and now a Markham man brings the horse in."

"He must want Gid Markham to see the horse!"

"Evidently," Roger said. "Three Markham men got away from the gunfight, and that sorrel will prove the fight was with our men."

Patricia said, "Gid's mother met me on the trail and told me that last night Gid promised to keep peace with us if not provoked."

"What Mexican trick—?"

"Not a trick," Patricia said quickly. "Consuela Markham was a Rivera, Roger. Her family has been in this country for generations. They were the *ricos*, at the top, proud. She was a mother, afraid for the only son she has left if there's more trouble."

Roger's cool voice lacked sympathy. "The woman has had enough years to stop trouble. Why talk about it now?"

"You'd have to know how her husband, Amos Markham, ruled their marriage. Consuela Markham was Mexican— reared to respect and obey her husband. Amos ignored her and bound his son to himself. He filled Gid with his hatred of the Kilgores." Patricia hesitated. "Amos even named his son Gideon. Do you know what it means?"

Roger was impatient. "What woman's foolishness now?"

"I met the *padre* on the trail one day," Patricia said slowly. "We talked of the Markhams, and Father Philippe told me that Gideon is a name from the Hebrew, and means 'a hewer-down.' And Amos Markham reared Gid that way— to hew down and destroy the Kilgores."

Roger's laugh was a short bark of derision. "What foolishness! I suppose Amos and Matt mean something also."

"The *padre* said Matthew means 'the gift of the Lord.' And Amos means 'one who bears a burden.' " And, when Roger stared at her, Patricia said steadily, "Amos Markham knew his Bible. Think how it comes out, Roger. . . . Amos, who 'bears the burden' reared his son as the 'hewer-down' of 'the gift of the Lord.' "

"Women and their ideas!" said Roger, and his sardonic amusement brought a flush to Patricia's cheeks.

"Don't laugh about Gid Markham!" Patricia flashed. "Or the promise he made to his mother last night!" She drew a breath. "If our men have had a gunfight with Gid's men, his promise is wiped out. Gid will be more vindictive than ever."

A man rode past at a jolting trot. A dogfight was clamoring in the distance. Roger had sobered. "Where's this sorrel horse now?"

"José Sanchez," Patricia said, "is bringing the horse in with the burro string. This man Clay Mara didn't look under the mane. I don't think he knows who owns the sorrel. Gid hasn't seen the horse. And you weren't there, Roger. You haven't even seen the three men."

"So?" said Roger narrowly.

Patricia slanted a glance up. "Don't ask questions, so you honestly won't know. I'll be at the hotel in an hour or so, unless I'm delayed."

"Pat—"

"Men," said Patricia, "make trouble—and women have to pick up the pieces."

Sternly Roger said, "This isn't—"

"Consuela Markham," Patricia said, "would go with me if she were here. If this man Mara asks questions, he can talk to me!"

9

Travis watched Pat Kilgore walk away, slender under the small chihuahua sombrero of straw which Pat preferred to the prim bonnets and frilly millinery of other young women. She could be tender and feminine in a way Travis had never known in a woman. He forced his thoughts to Grady Doyle, who had taken the sorrel gelding.

What had the fellow done? A fight. A wounded man. Possible trouble with Gid Markham too soon. Temper was dark in Travis as he started for the office of the *Soledad Beacon,* and the redheaded Dorothy Strance, who might know more about this business than she had told Patricia.

Black letters on the front window of the small frame building west of the plaza said:

THE BEACON

D. Strance, Editor.   *Notary.*   *Job Printing.*

The young widow seemed to know everything that happened in a hundred miles. She printed scathing items which would bring violence to a male editor. And she must be aware that she was in the bursting prime of her womanhood, desirable and needing a man. Travis drew a deeper breath as he stepped inside.

Behind a wooden counter, whittled on the edge and darkened by inky fingers, was a small hand press and a job press, stone forms, tables, and wall shelves holding paper stock. A gaunt printer wearing an eyeshade, ink-smudged canvas apron and paper cuffs was working intently at the type rack, composing-stick in hand.

D. Strance sat behind the counter at an old roll-top desk against the right wall. Her pencil lifted from a pad of paper as she looked up. Her question, "Are you from San Francisco, Mr. Travis?" was so casual that he almost said, "Yes." Travis laid his hat carefully on the counter and smiled. "I came up the Mississippi from New Orleans to St. Louis, ma'am, and then to New Mexico. One day I hope to see California."

After leaving California, he had traveled east to St. Louis, registered from New Orleans and converted his cash money into St. Louis Exchange. No person in New Mexico could say otherwise.

Regret crinkled the widow's forehead. "I hoped you were the R. Travis with an account in a San Francisco bank, so I could print it."

Uneasiness caught Travis. Holding the smile, he said, "What's worth printing about a bank account in San Francisco?"

"I subscribe to a San Francisco paper, and often we reprint stories from it." She was searching through penciled copy, letters, clippings. "Last night, in an old issue, I noticed a story about the South Bay Bank in San Francisco. And the name of R. Travis in it."

53

"A common name, ma'am."

"Not," said D. Strance, "if you were the man. Our readers enjoy stories about people they know. After I printed that paragraph about your gift of a hundred dollars to the *padre,* so many people spoke to me about it."

It was an effort to lean casually on the counter, smiling, while the woman chattered. *The South Bay Bank.* Travis started to sweat.

"Here it is!" said D. Strance, plucking out a newspaper clipping.

Travis wanted to bend over the counter and snatch the clipping from her. . . . And he had to stand smiling, fingers of his left hand straining on the counter edge as she read aloud from the clipping.

"It's headed 'Bold Abduction,'" said D. Strance, "and says, 'William Campbell, Cashier of the South Bay Bank, was abducted from his office today by a stranger who had attempted to cash a forged draft against an account in the name of R. Travis. Alerted by the teller, Mr. Campbell engaged the man in conversation while clerks summoned police. The stranger became alarmed, reached to a weapon in his coat pocket, and ordered Mr. Campbell to inform clerks outside the office door that a mistake had been made. Mr. Campbell was forced to accompany the man to a waiting carriage.'"

D. Strance chuckled. "Can't you see him marching out of the bank?"

"Yes," Travis said. His mouth was drying.

She read on: "'While being driven away from the bank, Campbell discovered that the apparent weapon in the stranger's coat was a straight-stemmed pipe.'"

D. Strance said with amusement, "Marching the cashier out past the clerks and customers with only a pipe in his pocket."

Travis could see it. Vividly he could see Campbell's walnut-paneled office and the big marble and gilt banking room on Montgomery Street in San Francisco. His voice sounded flat. "Did they catch the fellow?"

D. Strance said, "Catch a rascal who could do that with only a pipe in his pocket?" She read on.

" 'Sighting a patrolman, Campbell leaped out, shouting for help. A confederate in coachman's livery drove the carriage recklessly around the next corner away from the hue and cry. Police are searching the city and establishments on the Barbary Coast for the two desperadoes.' "

D. Strance said, "Whistles blowing. People shouting. Men running. And the man riding comfortably away with his pipe. It would have made a nice story if the bank account in the name of R. Travis had been yours."

She'd print it in bold type. The careful, smiling comment Travis made took effort to get out naturally.

"Someone else's account. Mind if I show that clipping to Matt Kilgore?"

"Since you're not the man, there's no use reprinting it." D. Strance went back to her swift writing as Travis walked out with the clipping. . . . And some moments later she paused and said aloud, "Now what did he want? He never did say."

Her printer made a dry reply as his hand flew between type rack and composing-stick. "He never got a chanct to say."

"That story with the name R. Travis has been on my mind." D. Strance's pencil tapped her even teeth. "Hank, the doctor says that wounded man will pull through, if the wound doesn't get infected. You know Ira Bell, don't you?"

"Busted many a bottle with the old buzzard."

"Bust another for the *Beacon*," said D. Strance inelegantly. "See if you can get Ira Bell to tell what happened. Everything."

"You hinted," said Hank, setting type steadily, "that them three are workin' for Gid Markham."

"I think so. And we know there was shooting." D. Strance made aimless marks on her pad and frowned. "I never saw a tougher-looking character than that roughneck calling himself Clay Mara who snored on my shoulder on the way in."

"Your shoulder," Hank said dryly, "don't look damaged. Time some man got a head on it. Though a feller who'd snore on a lady's shoulder ain't a lively prospect."

"Hank! This isn't the Bonanza! Or—or—"

"Or Carrie Plunkett's place out toward the stamp mill," Hank said calmly, setting type swiftly. "You're a growed-up girl, Miz Strance, purty an' tantalizin' to the men, even dressin' plain like you do an' tryin' to hide it."

"Hank!" said D. Strance, flushing.

"You got a little girl needs a daddy," Hank said. "Time you quit actin' like a pretty icicle on the Christmas tree."

"You know I'll never——"

"Don't take a stand a likely man can't rope you off of. You want I should bust a bottle with this here Clay Mara, too?"

"The *Beacon*," said D. Strance, "will buy all the bottles needed to start that one talking. He's——" She brooded. "The man's dangerous, Hank. It came off him like a reek."

"No man who comes walkin' in like he done gives off a vi'let smell," said Hank, unimpressed. "Try him when he gets outa the barber shop an' ain't snorin' in your ear—which'd rile any woman."

"Hank! I really mean——"

"I know," Hank said, type clicking rapidly into his metal composing-stick. "Well, we'll see. Strangers git fooled acrost a bottle by my ganted look. They keep tellin' 'emselves 'til they fall flat that it ain't possible I'm sittin' there sociable, talkin' away, givin' 'em two fer one."

Roger Travis's face had a stiff feel as he walked back to the corner of the plaza. It could have been an ordinary thief who had tried to get money from the account of R. Travis in the South Bay Bank. . . . But suppose the man had not been some shifty stranger off the San Francisco streets? Travis suspected he was not.

He had been certain that the real Roger Travis was dead. Now it seemed that the man must be alive, and had returned to San Francisco and tried to draw money from his account. Only the real Roger Travis would have presented a draft in the South Bay Bank with such confidence.

And the fellow was free now, knowing what had happened, and undoubtedly hunting the man who had taken over his name and all that he had.

Travis had been a lone wolf. He had always jeered at

weakness. But now, suddenly, he caught himself scanning every man in sight. He had never seen the real Roger Travis. Any stranger could be the man. *And the real Travis would know him.* Here in the Soledad country, the name was riveted on him. And most of the money was committed here now. He couldn't leave.

Sweating tension was building in Travis as he started across the plaza to Ledfesser's Mercantile to buy a gun and strap it on while he tried to think this out.

10

In Doctor Paul Halvord's sprawling adobe house west of the Soledad plaza, Clay Mara stood red-eyed and groggy while Howie Quist lay stripped to the waist on a narrow table covered with white oilcloth.

The lanky young doctor's big-knuckled, awkward looking hands were marvelously deft and gentle as they washed, probed, cut and sewed Howie's wounded side. Under his unruly hair, the young doctor's rawboned, craggy face was cheerful and his comments made even Howie grin weakly.

Howie was a tough bucket, the young doctor said, slapping Howie's bare shoulder. Had a stave punctured and had leaked too much. But the hole was plugged now and Howie would fill up again. . . . The doctor had been flicking professional glances at Clay. Behind the house was a spare room, Doctor Halvord said. Why not go back there and rest?

It was a small outside room with a floor of smooth dried mud and walls whitened neatly with *yeso*. Restfully cool and quiet as Clay sat on the rough plank cot and wearily tussled boots off swollen feet. A blue-tailed lizard whisked in from outside and froze on the window ledge, beady eyes watching Clay strip off socks and grunt with relief as cool air laved hot, blistered feet.

Civilized hooraw of soap, razor and clean clothes could

wait until sleep gave alertness to deal with the fellow who was calling himself Roger Travis. Hard humor bent Clay's mouth as he dropped back on the lumpy pallet in his clothes and visualized the man's stunned surprise. His grimy mouth was still grinning faintly when sleep came in a sodden wave. . . .

He was stretched inertly on the cot when rusty door hinges creaked. Instinct drove Clay into movement before his eyes opened. A startled, "Hold it!" reached him as his eyelids opened.

While his head had lifted, his hand had cocked and aimed the revolver he had left inside the top of his pants. In the open doorway a rigid figure held empty hands at chest level as Clay thickly demanded, *"Who're you?"*

"Gid Markham! You sent for me!"

Clay grunted and swung bare feet to the dirt floor and laid the revolver on the pallet. He pushed fingers through dusty hair, blinked puffy eyes, and yawned, trying to come awake. "You lost eighty-two horses at the Red Rock Tanks," Clay said shortly. "Now you worry about it."

Markham was younger than Clay had expected, wiry and broad-chested, wearing sober black. A thin, clean-chiseled face tightened to taut angles as Markham stared with suspicion at the red kerchief still around Clay's neck, the grimy shirt, unbuttoned coat, worn wool pants, all still dusty from the howling sandstorm yesterday.

"You pulled that gun fast," said Markham brusquely.

"Knock before you walk in on a stranger," Clay said dryly. He yawned again and asked, "Why'd you send an old man like Ira Bell up in the Navajo country for horses? He's too old."

Markham shrugged. "My mother knew Ira when she was a girl. He's been a good man. He wanted to go. Why let him feel useless now?"

Clay eyed with new interest the thin, chiseled face with its touch of arrogance and pride. "I see," said Clay, dryly again, and he had a new opinion of this Gid Markham after the revealing statement. "Seven men," Clay said, "were waiting for us in the sandstorm up on the ledges by the Red Rock Tanks. They wanted the horse herd. But they tried to

58

get us, too, after old Bell shouted that the horses were yours. They acted like they knew you."

"Most thieves know me," said Gid Markham curtly. "They knew my father, Amos Markham, too. Knew him from Old Mexico to the Big Colorado. We've hunted thieves down, hung 'em and shot 'em until they know."

With humorous irony, Clay said, "That way?"

"That way," said Gid Markham. "What happened at the Red Rocks?"

He sat on the end of the cot, resting a wiry, hard hand on a knee as he listened intently. His thin, dark face tightened over the pinto gelding callously shot as it tried to get up to water. Approval burned in the black eyes at Clay's handling of the camp guard, the furious slashing of saddle cinches and stirrup leathers. Markham's scowl set at the final ambush by one man at the lonely lava dike in the first dawn.

"So I walked in," Clay finished.

"And you've kept quiet about it?"

"Bell said he met a drifter up north, and spoke to the man of coming south soon with his horse herd," Clay said calmly. "That talk must have gotten to someone. The bunch at the Red Rocks knew we were coming. They must have friends here in Soledad. I kept quiet until you heard."

Markham's spur chains chinked softly as he got to his feet. Legs spread, hands adjusting the heavy cartridge belt under his coat, Markham thought over what he had heard.

"See any faces at all?" he inquired keenly.

"I saw the camp guard's face." Clay's slow smile of anticipation considered a thought. "The big fellow who seemed to be head of the bunch yelled *raafle,* instead of rifle. With my back turned and my eyes closed, if I hear that *raafle,* again, I'll have him nailed."

Gid Markham said, "Rifle—*raafle . . . raafle?*"

"Close enough," Clay said. "And I've got one of their horses, a sorrel gelding with a blaze and white stocking. I didn't notice the brand. Couple of Mexicans packing ore on burros are bringing him in. They work for Pat Kilgore, I think."

Temper and suspicion leaped into Markham's black eyes. "You know Pat Kilgore?"

59

"She was the first one I saw," said Clay shortly. "She turned her horse out from the road to meet us. A Mrs. Strance followed in her buggy, bringing the two Mexicans. I heard their names—and whose business is it who I know? Happens I never saw the Kilgore girl before, though."

"My mistake." Markham pushed his hat back off the damp hairline and stood thinking. "Ira Bell went north quietly with his silver for trading, so he wouldn't be followed. No honest man around here should know anything about it, even now. We'll keep it that way. I'll ride fast to the Red Rocks with enough men to hang that bunch if we corner them."

"And what will the sheriff be doing while you go hunting and hanging?" Clay inquired with irony.

Markham's shrug dismissed it as a useless question. "The sheriff," said Markham indifferently, "will be a hundred and fifty miles away, around his courthouse in Socorro, where he usually stays."

Clay considered that. "No law around here?" he asked with interest.

"A town marshal, and a deputy, for what he's worth when he's around. He'll thank me for this." Markham pulled off his hat and smoothed damp hair. "You are a stranger, Mara. We settle our own troubles out this way."

"I run to that myself," Clay said. "And if you ride near that lava dike, Howie's saddle and mine are there. I don't know where Bell's horse gave out. Oh—and bury that man at the lava."

Markham nodded carelessly and swung on out with haste. Clay was closing the door behind him when he heard footsteps and waited. It was the doctor, his craggy young face regretful.

"Sorry, Mara. Gid insisted on waking you."

"I wanted him to. How are Howie and the old man?"

"They're asleep." Halvord's keen eyes were curious. "You had another visitor I turned away—Roger Travis."

Clay kept his voice casual. "And who is Travis?"

Paul Halvord's smile came instinctively. "Fine chap. He's made friends everywhere."

"Who is he?"

"Roger Travis was Dick Kilgore's partner in Central America," Halvord said. "Both the partners sent money to Matt Kilgore to buy cattle for their joint account, and hold on Matt's ranch for the increase. Dick was killed down there in an accident, and Travis came here to dispose of his share of the cattle."

Clay grinned at the idea. "Does he think I'll buy his cattle?"

Halvord smiled, too. "Roger's investing in the Kilgore ranch and planning to stay, evidently. Gossip has it that Dick's sister changed his mind. Travis lost a wife rather tragically about two years ago. Now he seems to be finding happiness here."

"I see you like the man, too."

"Everyone does." Halvord's look took on a faintly guarded expression. "Roger seemed under some strain. He's never worn a gun, but he had one on today." Halvord hesitated. "I shouldn't speak of it. I'm a doctor and don't take sides. But you men are under my treatment and you're Markham men."

"Not Howie. Not me. We don't work for anyone."

Halvord's rawboned young face took on a puzzled expression. "My mistake," he said finally. "Gid said all three of you were his men. You know, I suppose, that there's bad blood between the Markhams and the Kilgores, which naturally includes Roger Travis now?"

"Markham didn't mention Travis. I'm a stranger here."

Halvord was rueful. "None of my business. If Roger Travis comes back, d'you want to see him?"

"Some other time, Doctor. I'll be asleep."

Clay was thoughtful as he closed the door and sat on the edge of the cot, musing on what he had just learned. . . . Little law in this Soledad country. . . . Travis had friends everywhere. . . . The man was investing heavily in the Kilgore ranch. . . . And the fellow was still trading on Vicky's death.

Clay dropped back on the hard shuck pallet and stared unseeingly at the log *vigas* overhead. The ache of loneliness for Vicky came back. He was thinking of Travis in simmering anger when utter weariness came down upon him again and sleep gave him peace.

61

11

In a sweating hour, walking alone on the outskirts of Soledad past barking dogs and shrilling children, Travis faced
the full dangerous knowledge that the real Roger Travis
must be alive and was undoubtedly hunting him. And the
man would eventually come here to Soledad.

How much time was left?

Tension crawled in Travis as he faced the trap he was
in. He had meant to sell the cattle and leave quickly. . . .
And he had stayed, planning a future in this country far
bolder than anything he had visualized in the past. Most of
his money was committed here now—and the tell-tale name
of Roger Travis was riveted on him.

Anger and a kind of helpless despair came as Travis
realized the scant choices he had now, and all that he stood
to lose. He could vanish, leaving behind most of his money
and abandoning all thought of Patricia Kilgore . . . or he
could risk a week, two weeks more here—*did he have that
much time?*—and get out with what money he could re-
cover, and probably with Patricia.

Or . . .

Travis halted by an empty corral. A new and flaring hope
held him motionless. There were other kinds of traps. The
real Roger Travis could walk into a trap. *If the fellow were
killed . . .*

When Travis walked slowly back to the Boston House on
the southwest corner of the plaza, he was a more dangerous
man than he had ever been. He was waiting to kill a man he
had never seen and would not know when they met. But the
man would know him. Day and night he would have to live
with the grinding, watchful tension.

Patricia Kilgore had not returned. Travis was closely

inspecting the hotel register for strangers in town when the smiling clerk said, "A young lawyer name of Rapburn got off the Socorro stage, Mr. Travis, and hired a buggy and drove out to the ranch to see you."

Travis managed his usual warm smile and thought a moment. "When Miss Kilgore comes in, tell her I've gone back to the ranch to see the man."

He held the smile as he walked across the plaza to Ledfesser's Store. An hour ago, buying the revolver and gunbelt now strapped under his coat, he had bought a carbine also and left it in the store. He rammed the carbine into the empty saddle scabbard in a vicious mood of finality, and rode out of the plaza without looking back. And almost immediately he came upon the one man he least wished to see while planning to kill a man in cold blood.

Father Philippe, the sun-browned little Franciscan *padre,* was vigorously driving nails into the gate in the low adobe wall enclosing the bare yard of his small church. Hammer in hand, sleeves of his brown, belted robe turned back, the *padre's* smiling greeting forced Travis to pull up.

"I see you have started to carry guns now, Mr. Travis."

Travis barely managed a civil, "Everyone does."

"A custom which would be alarming in my native France," the *padre* said cheerfully.

"This isn't France," said Travis carelessly. He was lifting the reins to ride on when the *padre's* gesture held him.

Kindly now, and earnest, Father Philippe said, "Your generous gift some time ago has not been forgotten. Daily, Mr. Travis, you and your departed wife have been remembered in prayers. Particularly that you may be granted all that you deserve."

"Don't bother any more," Travis said shortly. "I'll get what I deserve myself. Always have, always will."

The *padre's* small smile was serene as he rolled a sleeve of the brown robe higher.

"Prayers are never wasted, Mr. Travis." And when Travis shrugged and put his horse on, the *padre* called the friendly parting of the native Mexicans, *"Con Dios*—with God."

Unreasonable anger, and again a small chill of foreboding, stayed with Travis as he shook the horse into a fast lope. He

63

had been a fool some time ago to carelessly hand the *padre* the hundred dollars for luck. Gambler's luck. And now, while he was planning to kill a man, he was being linked in prayers with that man's dead wife. Travis had never considered himself superstitious—but the smiling little *padre* made him so now. Some things were best left alone.

In that mood, his anger turned to the trouble which Grady Doyle and his men seemed to have made with Gid Markham. What had happened, Travis still did not know. He had tried to talk to the stranger named Clay Mara, and the doctor had refused to disturb the exhausted, sleeping man.

Mara and his two companions had reached Soledad. There was a chance that Grady Doyle's bunch had returned. But when Travis rode down through trees and brush once more and sighted the low, slab-rock line cabin again, deserted quiet still hung over the place. In a memo-book, Travis wrote with slashing strokes: *Doyle—see me at the ranch at once.* He weighted the note under an empty bottle on the littered table inside the cabin, and rode on at a faster pace.

And now the great sun-flooded draws, the long, sheltering ridges and soft haze of distance on far mountains began to take on new values. So did the Kilgores when Travis thought about them. Matt Kilgore and Patricia Kilgore.

In the journal of the real Roger Travis, he had read with casual derision of the man's high hopes and eager plans. And of the man's young wife in Wyoming who had been a part of it.

Something which Travis still did not quite understand had happened to him here in this Soledad country. He had found his own high hopes and eager plans—and the girl to share them. And he had found more than that, Travis realized as he skirted the last piñon and juniper covered ridge, and saw across the smiling grass flats the distant Kilgore ranchhouse. He had come cynically to sell cattle and depart, and now that he faced losing everything, it came to him that the house ahead was the only place he had ever really been glad to come back to.

He was wanted here. Without meaning to, he had become part of a warm-hearted family. Here he had found all that the real Roger Travis had found in Wyoming and had lost.

And mockery filled the thought that, while using the other man's name and identity, he himself might lose everything here.

The tension of what he faced, and what he must do, caught Travis again as he sighted Jim Rapburn's buggy in the ranch yard behind the house, and Matt Kilgore out in the open talking to the young Socorro lawyer. Travis put his horse into a final run, planning how best now to use this lawyer he had hired some time ago.

When Travis swung down by the two men, Matt Kilgore's chuckle greeted him. "You got sensible an' bought a gun, I see," Matt said.

"I took your advice about Gid Markham," Travis said lightly, and it pleased Matt as he intended. Travis turned to Rapburn. "Jim, I heard in town that I'd missed you."

Jim Rapburn's handshake was warm. Shorter than Travis, Rapburn's gray suit, narrow-brimmed hat, white linen shirt and soft calfskin shoes marked him a rather prosperous townsman.

Matt Kilgore broke in. "Roger, lemme see you use that new gun." Matt's rope-scarred hand pointed to a newly peeled corner post of the nearest corral. "See that rosin-spot halfway up?"

Good-naturedly Travis said, "Matt, I can use a gun."

A grim smile touched Matt's weather-scoured face. "Come a day that rosin-spot might be Gid Markham's gun muzzle. Or one of Gid's men. Show me we won't lose you then, son."

Without haste Travis drew and fired—and, in the instant, his face hardened as he thought of the real Roger Travis. He drove two bullets fast at the post.

The reports slammed across the yard and echoed back from the low, timbered ridge to the north. Matt peered at the post and chuckled with satisfaction.

"Either one'd stop a man." His callused hand dropped on Travis's shoulder. "Ain't much call to worry about you. I got things to do now. We'll get together later." Matt walked away.

The peculiar expression on the young lawyer's face brought Travis's amused comment. "Jim, you look like you've seen a ghost."

65

Jim Rapburn had thoughtful eyes and sensitive features still untanned by the southwestern sun. "I was watching your face when you fired," Rapburn said slowly. "You meant it." His smile was forced. "I saw Gid Markham killed just then."

"Not Markham," Travis said, and the tension caught him again as he thought of the target that had been in his mind. He changed the subject, eyeing the young lawyer critically. "You look well and prosperous."

Rapburn's flush was self-conscious as he glanced down at his new gray suit. "Does something for a man to have money in his pocket and dress like he's successful."

Cynically, Travis said, "Does more to other people when they know he's successful. They like him; they come running to please him."

"Like I jump to please you," said Rapburn wryly.

"Jim! I wasn't suggesting anything like that!" Travis could be warmly convincing. He left his horse there with reins on the ground and they fell into slow step together.

Rapburn's glance went about the wide, busy ranch yard. "This looks like a fort making ready for a campaign. Supplies stacking up, men coming and going. Wagons in and out."

"Something like that," Travis said. He handed over a cigar and bit the end off another. They were good cigars, the best of the Bonanza stock in Soledad.

Rapburn sniffed the tobacco appreciatively. Travis got his smoke going and absently broke the match at right angles. They were both, he suspected, thinking of the same thing—of how Jim Rapburn, the young lawyer, out from the East for his health, had sat in Socorro, the county seat of this vast Socorro county, pockets empty, suits threadbare, until Travis had come to him with a handsome retainer. Rapburn might even be aware that he had been selected because he was new in the Territory, without old allegiances, and needed money desperately enough to serve a well-paying client with all effort.

"The surveyors," Rapburn said slowly, "are back in Socorro. Everything is about ready." He seemed troubled. "As your lawyer, I must ask if it's wise to expand Kilgore's ranch as planned."

"Matt's decision," said Travis calmly. "I'm only backing him."

It was a fiction which even Matt believed, and Rapburn's comment was sincere. "A son couldn't be doing more for Kilgore."

"I feel almost like a son," Travis said; and, in a way, he did feel so, he mused, as they strolled past workmen enlarging the bunkhouse.

On the north side of the yard, Matt's booming voice was audible. Rapburn's glance that way was still troubled. "Does Kilgore realize the trouble he'll have with Gideon Markham?" Rapburn asked uncomfortably. "Markham isn't a weakling."

Travis spoke with scorn as they walked on beyond the last corrals. "Markham is no worry." *The worry was the stranger who had bluffed his way out of the South Bay Bank with a pipe stem.* Tightly cautious, he said, "You're my lawyer, not Kilgore's lawyer. I own cattle here. My money is in this ranch. How quickly could I sell everything for cash?"

"You couldn't."

"You might say then I'm trapped in all this now."

"In a way," Rapburn agreed.

"Means staying with it," Travis said. And, with the bald choice on him again, his long-boned, rugged face hardened. "Ever have big plans, big dreams, Jim?"

Young Rapburn's smile was wry. "More than my share. There's been so much to dream about that I haven't got."

"I came here to sell my cattle," Travis said, "and I found a chance at the future which few men will ever have." In spite of the sweating strain which would not leave now, enthusiasm sharpened Travis's words. "The railroad is going to cross the Territory toward California. Cattle can be shipped out. Settlers will come. More mines will open. Towns will grow. The man who makes friends now, and digs in and spreads out, will have a chance for wealth beyond anything this Territory has ever known." Travis looked at the gray ash lengthening on his cigar and added coolly, "And men who work with him will grow big, too."

Under his breath Jim Rapburn said, "Is that why Kilgore is ready to fight even the Markhams to expand now?"

"The Markhams," said Travis impatiently, "don't count. Old Amos Markham was in the Army with Matt. After they got out, Amos married a Mexican girl from one of the old native families. He was kingpin, and he started to spread over everything in sight. When Matt Kilgore married and started to ranch in this same country, Amos tried to crowd him out. Even raised his son, Gid Markham, to fight Matt. Gid Markham almost had Matt on his knees when I came here."

"I've heard so," Rapburn murmured.

"Amos Markham," said Travis scornfully, "ran the country around here like an old-time hacienda, everyone on it peons of his. Gid Markham wants it to stay that way. He can't see what's ahead. If he makes trouble, he'll be pushed aside." Travis drew on his cigar and said evenly, "Matt might not live to see it all happen. But this ranch will and his daughter will."

Full understanding came keenly into Rapburn's glance. "I'd forgotten Miss Kilgore," Rapburn said, smiling faintly. He drew a slow breath. "If you follow through with this, you'll end up one of the biggest men in the Territory—or a dead man."

"My money is in it. I can't get out now if I want to. And I don't intend to lose or get killed," Travis said with hardening calmness.

12

When Clay Mara came awake in the little outside room at Doctor Halvord's house, mote-spangled sunlight through the open window made him stare unbelievingly. He felt sharp and alive and ravenously hungry as he crossed the cold, hard mud floor on bare feet and opened the door. By the sun, it was long after seven in the morning. In rumpled, sand-filled clothes, he'd slept nearly twenty hours. In the distance across the low roofs of town the mountains lifted, purple-shadowed under the cloudless sky. Yesterday those mountains had mocked his exhausted, grimly stubborn will to reach the fellow who was calling himself Roger Travis.

Clay thought of the man in detached anticipation as he walked around the doctor's quiet adobe house and turned toward the plaza. Yesterday the town had been a tired blur. Now he saw that they built mostly of adobe here, and the town sprawled away from the sunny plaza without much pattern.

Sun-roofs extended over the plaza walks. Native New Mexicans, dark-skinned for the most part and leisurely, were numerous. Ledfesser's seemed to be the largest store. Clay bought what he needed there, and crossed the plaza again past a tangle of Indians just arrived—bucks, squaws, children standing by scraggly ponies. The long, gay-colored skirts of the squaws marked them as friendly Navajos.

Barber Shop—Baths.

Clay walked in, and in a back room he soaked luxuriously in a tin tub, lathering the desert out of his hair, digging grit out of ears and eye corners. Clay sang from sheer animal vigor and knowledge that the long trail ended here. He scoured the towel furiously over glowing skin and cording muscles, opened the bundle from Ledfesser's and pulled on new clothes, keeping only the sweat-stained leather money belt and comfortable old boots.

Men were loitering in the barber shop. While lather foamed over his beard bristles, Clay asked casually if Roger Travis were in town. Travis was not. But the question started them talking of Travis. Of the money the man had. Of the way he was helping Matt Kilgore. Friendly talk. They liked Travis; they respected the fellow.

Clay speculated on what they'd say if he told them he was really Roger Travis. They'd jeer, he knew. The Kilgores had accepted Travis and were backing him. In this remote part of New Mexico, with little law, Travis could kill an armed stranger and, with his money and new friends, get

69

away with it. And, at the first suspicion, Travis would. Clay had no doubt of it now.

The barber's mirror showed a new man, hair trimmed, dark face cleanly smooth. The new wool pants, canvas jacket, gray cotton shirt and fresh red kerchief felt luxurious as Clay walked from the barber shop to the sign he had already marked.

Ah Wing—Eats.

Ah Wing was back in his kitchen clattering pans as Clay sat at a scrubbed pine table. The plump waitress grew wide-eyed, fascinated as she brought coffee, hot biscuits, steak, eggs, fried potatoes, more coffee, more steak. . . . "More coffee, ma'am—"

The waitress asked, "When'd you eat last, mister?"

Clay grinned over the bite of steak on his fork. "Long time ago."

"If you ever et before, there wouldn't be that much room," she said with conviction.

Clay asked directions and walked to a feed corral, and there was no sorrel horse waiting for him. He tried the Star Livery and Feed, east of the plaza corner, a long, low adobe barn with a runway through the center. In one of the stalls, a young Mexican hostler in waist overalls and red-checked shirt was wiping a horse with a sack. Teeth flashed at Clay's question. "You want horse the lady left?" They walked back to the corral behind the barn. "The black one, *señor.*"

Clay rested elbows on a corral bar and eyed the black gelding across the corral. Not a cull. Short coupled like the sorrel, with a look of soundness and bottom. Over a shoulder, in Spanish, Clay asked, "Miss Kilgore brought that black one in? For Clay Mara?"

And back in Spanish, cheerfully, "In the office is the paper of sale. He is one good horse, no? *Sala'o!*"

Clay said, *"Sala'o?"* inquiringly.

"Salty—*salado,*" explained the boy. Slender, good-natured, his dark eyes glinted with amusement. "We say '*sala'o.*'"

Clay dropped back into English. "Let's see that bill of sale," he said dryly.

He was rueful when the boy left him. Should have guessed

70

that the Spanish he had learned in Old Mexico and on south would be different. Like New Orleans talking to Boston. . . . And Travis, too, would probably know the difference by now. Best not admit knowing Spanish from now on. The boy returned with a brown unsealed envelope. Silently Clay read the enclosure.

I hereby sell and transfer to Clay Mara for value received all rights and ownership in the black gelding branded MK on neck, right side. Patricia Kilgore.

The slanting pen strokes were impersonal, explaining nothing. The bill of sale was as coolly antagonistic, in a way, as Patricia Kilgore herself had been yesterday. She was close to Travis. She was at odds with Gid Markham. The missing sorrel had been taken from the men at Red Rocks. Clay put the paper back into the envelope.

"Where can I find Mrs. Strance who owns the newspaper?" he inquired.

"West," the boy said. "Across plaza. Is little house. Flowers, sandpile in front."

"How about renting a saddle and gun boot?"

Clay took the rope from the boy and went into the corral and brought the black out. Preoccupied, trying to fit bits of this mystery together, he stepped into the saddle.

Sala'o—salty.

The exploding jump and spin almost threw him. The boy started to laugh. The grin Clay tried to give back was shaken off his face as he barely managed to get the plunging brute's head up and turned into the barn.

Thankful he'd hauled cinches tight, Clay rode the bucking, twisting black through the long shadowy runway of the barn. Only in the wide street outside did he get the hard mouth under control. The young hostler had run through the barn after him and was still laughing.

"Sala'o!" Clay called wryly, and swung the black toward the plaza, across it and on.

He found the sandpile; and the black gelding went falsely hipshot and placid when Clay stepped off. With a jaundiced look, Clay warned, "Don't count on it next time."

71

It was a neat little house with tan-colored earthen walls washed by infrequent rains into graceful, grooved patterns. Lush green of an irrigated garden was visible behind the house, with a row of tepeelike poles covered with climbing bean vines. And, to the right of the narrow front *portal,* under the reaching green branches of a cottonwood tree, a doll was kneeling in a board-enclosed sandpile. The doll's grubby hand waved as Clay opened the gate in the low picket fence and walked to her. A small, distressed lower lip was protruding.

Helplessly the doll said, "Wolf's nose felled off."

A tin basin held muddy water. She had been molding a damp sand image. Its nose had indeed fallen off. A tiny Chihuahua dog almost the color of the sand stood in one corner of the box and watched Clay with alert, pricked ears.

"Is that Wolf, ma'am?" Clay inquired with caution.

"He won't bite," said the doll reassuringly.

"Had me worried," Clay said with relief. He pushed back his hat and considered the problem. "Did you squeeze the sand tight?"

The doll's scrubbed, healthy little face was freckled and smeared with mud. Red hair was parted into two braids, each with a small bow of green ribbon. "I squoze," she said forlornly, "but it felled off."

"More water in the sand might help," Clay suggested. He stepped into the sandpile and dropped to a knee.

The doll leaned close, watching his hands work. Her dress and her apron were neatly ironed. Her question was hopeful. "Are you my daddy?"

"No, ma'am."

"He wented away," the doll said. "What's your name?"

"Clay Mara. What's yours?"

"Lucinda."

"That," said Clay admiringly, "is a pretty name." Carefully he pinched a new nose to an aggressive point.

"Gid Markham," the doll confided, "says Lucinda means sugar an' spice. He rides me on his horse."

"Ride your mother, too?" Clay asked, working on an ear.

The doll chortled. "Mommy's a big girl."

72

And an amused voice spoke on the house *portal*. "Do you children need a larger sandpile?"

Clay dipped hands into the basin and stood up, catching off his hat. "I used to be better at snow men, ma'am."

The Widow Strance's fresh cotton print dress was as plain today as yesterday, and her bright red hair was caught smoothly back. She was smiling without recognition as she walked to the sandpile, until he said, "I'm Clay Mara, ma'am."

Her eyes widened and grew guarded. Her comment was impersonal with amused irony. "Do you usually start the day playing in a sandpile, Mr. Mara?"

The doll said, "I like him, Mommy. Do you like him?"

Clay smiled at the Widow Strance's expression. "Don't answer, ma'am. I didn't stop here to be praised."

She flushed, and for a moment looked like an older copy of the doll, close to having her warm lower lip protrude in distressed uncertainty. Smiling, Clay pulled pipe and tobacco from his coat pocket. "I came to ask about my sorrel horse. Where is he?"

The Widow Strance's smooth face recovered composure. "José Sanchez brought your horse in. Ask at the feed corrals or the livery barn." She watched Clay thumb tobacco into the straight-stemmed pipe. Her mouth parted slightly.

Calmly, Clay said, "This black gelding was left at the Star Livery for me. Miss Kilgore left him, and a bill of sale for him. But I had a sorrel horse. I want him."

"Of course. And light your pipe, if you wish, Mr. Mara."

Clay did so, and reminded her, "You were the one who said that the sorrel would be brought into town."

"I thought he would be."

For a remembering moment, Clay looked at her shoulder where his grimy, unshaven face had sagged while he had slept, exhausted, in her buggy yesterday. She had been understanding about it, as a young widow could be. Now she seemed on guard against him, with speculation in her hazel eyes.

"Those two Mexicans work for Miss Kilgore," Clay said.

"Yes." In something like fascination, Mrs. Strance was watching the straight-stemmed pipe in his hand.

73

"That doesn't explain why a black horse arrived instead of the sorrel," Clay said coolly.

He was thinking of the way the Widow Strance's pliant young figure had tensed against him in the buggy yesterday when he had mentioned Gid Markham. And of what her small daughter had revealed about Markham. Mrs. Strance seemed to read the turn of his thoughts.

"Many things seem to need explaining," she said, watching him. "Gid Markham rode in at once and talked to you, and left town immediately. Then Gid gathered men and rode off on some urgent matter. But strangely, Mr. Mara, no one in town seems to know about it."

"Markham's business isn't mine," said Clay indifferently. "But if you're his friend, don't talk about what he's doing until you see him."

Her slight frown considered him. "What Gid is doing doesn't concern you?"

"No."

She was perplexed. "Why is Gid being secretive?"

"You seem to know all that happens," Clay reminded with his own irony. "Why don't you know more about my sorrel?"

"Why should the sorrel be so important?"

"Because, ma'am, someone seems to think he is important," Clay said. His smile came again. "I've never played in a sandpile with a sweeter young lady."

The doll's grubby hand waved as Clay turned to leave. He waved back. Mrs. Strance stood by her daughter and watched him short-rein the black gelding, slam into the saddle watchfully, and hold the edgy black brute with a hard bit. Only then did she lift her voice.

"Mr. Mara—when were you in California last?"

Clay's teeth clamped on the pipe stem. He halted the black's half-wheel, reined back, and took the pipe from his mouth. "I don't remember saying I was ever in California, ma'am."

"Not yesterday?" Mrs. Strance countered. "In the buggy, when you were almost asleep?"

Clay stared at her with a kind of shock. Had he blabbered

74

and mumbled, unawares, in that exhausted soddenness which had blanked out on her soft shoulder?

Her smile came, provocative, with an edge of mockery. Of a sudden, pretty as she was despite her plain dress and severely pinned hair, she took on threat and danger. The smile Clay forced was an effort. "A man can say anything in his sleep, ma'am."

She persisted. "You *have* been in California, haven't you? In San Francisco?"

Now Clay knew she was dangerous, and his own danger from this minute was acute. He kept the smile on tight lips. "Forgot something, haven't you, ma'am?"

"What, Mr. Mara?"

"You know everything that happens and print it," Clay reminded. "I'll read your paper, ma'am, and find out where I've been." He let the black spin out into the street, and he heard her confident promise.

"You will, Mr. Mara! You will!"

13

Doctor Paul Halvord was out. A plump Mexican housekeeper looked at Clay's dark, serious face and silently led him to the door of the patients' room. And, as Clay walked in, Howie Quist's indignant protest met him.

"How'm I gonna get outa here? They took my britches an' left me in a danged nightshirt!"

Howie was sitting in outrage on a cot, swathed in a blanket. On an adjoining cot, propped up on pillows, old Ira Bell looked ancient and dried-out behind his long bristle of gray beard stubble. But the old man's sunken eyes had regained alertness, and Howie's broad face had a trace of healthy color this morning.

75

Clay laughed at Howie's indignation. "Some Navajo squaw in the plaza might swap you a purple petticoat."

Ira Bell cackled from his pillows.

"I'll teach 'im Navvyjo. He can shake them shanks an' bargain fer a squaw, an' a hogan an' sheep t' herd."

"You two," said Howie sourly, "ain't funny."

Still smiling, Clay spoke to Ira Bell. "How does Mrs. Strance find out so many things?"

"Wimmen."

"What women? Patricia Kilgore?"

Interest and humor glinted in Bell's sunken eyes. "The widder git holt of somethin' she oughtn't about you?"

"Stop gabbling," Clay said. "I need to know."

"Told you wimmen," said Ira Bell again, grinning in his long scraggle of beard. "Wimmen fer two days' ride out, takin' note of ary thing that happens. They write in an' fetch in to the widder's paper all they git holt of. The widder prints it fer the other wimmen to keep up with an' gabble over. A passel of men peekin' through knotholes an' keyholes couldn't come up with half so much."

"I see," Clay said, and was no better off than he had been. "What happened to the widow's husband?"

"Apaches," said Bell briefly. "A burro freighter found him off the Socorro road. Couple months later the widder had her baby."

Clay nodded, and his sympathy was instant for the young widow who had carried on with spirit. "Gid Markham rode to the Red Rocks with men. He wants it kept quiet. And remember what I asked you yesterday?"

"I ain't fergot I owe you fer bringin' me in," said Ira Bell calmly. "You two come ridin' by fer Santa Fe an' I hired you. Don't know no more."

"Hold to it," Clay said. "Howie, can you make it outside the door?"

Howie said, "I'm good as I ever was!" He stood up and staggered. "Bed gets a man," Howie muttered. He draped the blanket around the long white nightshirt.

"Can't tell 'im from a Navvyjo," cackled Ira Bell again.

Howie glared at the old man and walked with visible effort out into the hall. Clay closed the door behind them and spoke thoughtfully. "Howie, that redheaded young widow just asked me when I was in San Francisco last. And yesterday, while I was asleep, Travis tried to see me. The doctor said Travis was wearing a gun for the first time."

"Oh-oh!" Howie muttered. His broad, unshaved face showed concern as he leaned for support against the whitened adobe wall. "It don't sound good," Howie said. "If that feller's got any idea who you are, Clay, he'll sure try to kill you on sight."

"No doubt of it."

Howie wiped a fold of the blanket across a glistening dew of weakness on his forehead.

"After we took off from that hollerin' bank cashier in San Francisco," Howie said, "I figured your story about this Travis was the pappy of tall ones. But I was messed into it, so I come along. Now you got the skunk cornered—an' he may be layin' for you this mornin'."

"I'll have to count on it," Clay agreed. "Another thing, our sorrel horse never reached town. The Kilgore girl left a black gelding instead at the livery barn. And a free bill of sale giving me the black."

Howie looked blank. Clay shrugged. "With Travis cornered now and maybe knowing who I am, I can't wait."

"Wait a few days 'til I can side you," Howie pleaded.

"Can't give him a chance, Howie, with him knowing that killing me will make him safe the rest of his life. I'm riding out to the Kilgore ranch now to look him over. I wanted you to know in case I don't get back."

Howie's dismayed concern held him silent for a moment. "I guess you'll go," Howie said finally. "Well—good luck."

From her front yard Dorothy Strance, disturbed and apprehensive, had watched the tall stranger named Mara enter the doctor's house. And a little later she watched from the *Beacon* office as he rode by.

The black gelding was fighting the bit. Straight and thoughtful in the saddle, Clay Mara was ignoring the horse. This morning, rested and alert, he looked younger. When he had knelt in the sandpile with his head close to her small daughter's bright braids, he had seemed a warm, friendly

77

stranger—until she had recognized him. Until she had remembered him yesterday—red-eyed, unshaven, his thick, harsh tones backed by a falsely humorous, steely quality.

Now, as Dorothy Strance stood behind the whittled counter in her office, Hank the printer spoke dryly behind her. "Likely lookin' young stranger, ain't he?"

Under her breath, Dorothy said, "He's the man named Clay Mara. Look at him, Hank. He means trouble. He's hard; he can be pitiless."

Through the *Beacon* window, the holstered gun under Mara's new canvas jacket was visible. The carbine he had carried tiredly in a grimy hand yesterday was in the leather scabbard under his leg. When he had stood up in the sandpile, he had adjusted a second revolver in the front of his shirt. Under the old hat, his mahogany-hued face was somber now. A remote look, a solitary look hung about him as he rode the fretting black gelding unhurriedly toward the plaza.

"So that's him?" said Hank with dry humor, moving to the counter. "No wonder you got riled at a likely hunk of man like him sleepin' on your shoulder."

Soberly Dorothy said, "Hank, he smokes a straight-stemmed pipe! Remember yesterday when Roger Travis asked for that clipping? And walked out without saying why he'd come in the office here?"

"You still thinkin' of that man in the San Francisco bank with a pipe?"

"Yes!"

Hank was bony and his shoulders stooped. Black printer's ink under his fingernails made Hank's hands look perpetually dirty. His glance now under the inky eyeshade was quizzical. "Ain't you makin' a lot out of a little?"

Thoughtfully Dorothy said, "You heard Travis deny ever having been in San Francisco. But he wanted the clipping. And half an hour ago this Clay Mara wouldn't admit anything at all about San Francisco." On her fingers, Dorothy ticked off points. "Mara walked in from a gunfight and wouldn't talk about it. But he sent for Gid Markham. And Gid rode off somewhere with armed men. Then Patricia Kilgore substituted that black horse for the sorrel horse that Mara had. They're all hiding something!"

78

"Who ain't?" said Hank.

"I think something we haven't suspected is happening under our noses!" said Dorothy with disturbed conviction. "And I think Clay Mara is going to the Kilgore ranch now. A dollar he is, Hank!"

"Not a beat-up dime agin your hunches," Hank declined. "Cost me too many times a'ready." Hank's sardonic look estimated her under the eyeshade. "Who you so stirred up about—Travis, this stranger or Gid Markham?"

Color, Dorothy knew, bloomed in her cheeks. "Gid can take care of himself. I'm concerned about Patricia Kilgore."

"That girl's home, safe enough."

Dorothy caught her straw hat off the desk top where she had tossed it when she came in.

"Hank! Hank! Are you blind? Have you forgotten what that girl's been through? Lost most of her family. Seen their ranch almost lost! And now Travis has brought happiness and hope to her. And to Matt Kilgore. If something happens now—"

"Where you going?" Hank inquired dubiously.

Flushed and pinning on her hat, Dorothy said, "I'm going to the *padre* who knows more than most people suspect. Then I'm going to the Kilgore ranch and cut through from there on the Piedras trail and talk with Gid Markham's mother!"

"Here we go again," said Hank, and he sounded resigned. " 'The Beacon,' " Hank quoted in sarcasm, " 'Lights the Way.' "

But when he was alone, Hank stood at the counter some moments. Finally he stripped off his eyeshade and went out also. Bony, stooped, Hank walked to Doctor Paul Halvord's house to visit sympathetically, shrewdly with old Ira Bell and the stranger named Howie Quist.

Yesterday Patricia Kilgore had been defiant about the stranger named Mara. . . . This morning her waking thoughts were uneasy. In the clear mirror of her bedroom dresser, the long black hair she was twisting and pinning on top of her head made her look taller. And, still taller behind her reflection, she could visualize the stranger bronzed and threatening behind his carbine sights in the dry wash. He had been surly, harsh; his hard hand had callously struck the wounded man in the face. And he had sent for Gid Markham to come to him.

The metallic clangor of the cookhouse triangle found Patricia at her own kitchen range, wearing her best apron with box-pleated bib and pocket. Cedar and pitch pine chunks were hissing and crackling; one stove plate was cherry red.

Last night her father and Roger Travis and the young Socorro lawyer had talked late in the room Matt used for an office. At times they had sounded serious. But when Matt's booming laughter had lifted, Patricia's grateful smile had come because of all Roger was doing for Matt.

This morning Patricia served them breakfast in the long, low-ceilinged kitchen of the house. Sunlight slanted cheerfully in on the tablecloth. The ham, eggs and biscuits were fragrant.

Matt had a pleased, faintly excited look. Once or twice young Jim Rapburn smiled at Patricia as if he shared some pleasant secret with her. When Rapburn glanced at Roger, the lawyer's thin, sensitive face flushed slightly with a queer, reckless expression. Like a man gambling when he wasn't really a gambler, Patricia thought.

When the men pushed back their chairs, Patricia's glance signaled Roger to stay. Stacking plates alone with Roger, she asked, "Did you tell Matt about the sorrel?"

Roger was amused as he stacked saucers.

"I'm not supposed to know about the sorrel or what you did yesterday," Roger reminded.

Patricia carried the plates to the sink, and looked out the window at the ranch road dwindling toward Soledad. "Suppose that man Mara comes here?"

"Tell him anything you planned," said Roger, joining her. "If he makes trouble, I'll take a hand."

"You always do these days," said Patricia under her breath. She looked out the window again. "When some of the first Spanish explorers came up the Rio Grande Valley, Roger, they ran out of food and water crossing the Jornado

—that dry stretch east of the Rio Grande they came to call the Journey of Death because so many have died there."

"History lesson?" Roger chuckled.

"They reached an Indian pueblo and were given corn and meat and named the place Socorro," Patricia said.

"Succor—help," Roger translated.

Patricia nodded. "Later on the pueblo moved to the west bank of the river, and the town that finally was there was still called Socorro. This county is Socorro. And to us you've been *socorro*, Roger. Help when it was needed."

Roger stood in silence, and Patricia had never felt closer to him. He was like one of her brothers, strong and reassuring as he slipped his arm naturally about her.

"Patricia!" She looked up and Roger kissed her. . . . And it was not a brotherly kiss.

Her first impulse was to push away. But her hands pressed the rough wool cloth of his blue coat, and held there as Roger kissed her again. Hungry, demanding . . . A glow ran through her and her pulses began to pound. Roger said unsteadily, "Pat! Pat!"

"You were married, Roger! The way you've talked about her—"

Roger's voice was strained. "All that is over. You and I count now, Pat." He kissed her again, roughly; and then, against her cheek, fiercely, "Pat, I need you."

Need you—Patricia caught at the steadying thought. Matt had needed someone like Roger. And she, too, had needed.

After a moment, Patricia put her arms around Roger. Cheek against his rough coat, she said, "We've all needed each other, haven't we?" And then all she could think of was an unsteady try at humor. "I suppose Matt will say, 'I've lost a daughter and gained a son.' "

Roger was jubilant. "I'll tell Matt now."

Patricia said, "I want to tell him." She added, "Alone."

Roger's arm held her close as they looked out the window. "No woman in the Territory will have more," Roger said with a kind of fierceness. "More money than you imagine! The future bigger than you suspect." He kissed her again. "Shall we ride in to the preacher today?"

The man . . . Patricia's laughter was firm. "Not today."

"Sometime this week then? We know what we want. Now!"

"I'll talk to Matt."

"Then I'll finish with Jim Rapburn, so he can start back to Socorro," Roger said. His final kiss was possessive.

When he was gone, Patricia looked about the kitchen. . . . Had her mother felt this way in Santa Fe, long ago, when she had met Matt?

Here in the kitchen, under the log *vigas* chocolate-brown from smoke and age, her mother had always seemed closer. Because that young and happy bride had made her first home under these *vigas*. In the deep stone fireplace, her young mother had cooked in smoke-sooted iron pots. And, as her mother had done, Patricia herself kept bright red chili peppers hanging in a corner. And strings of peeled squash and melon meats, dried Indian-style. And shriveled dried green chili and sun-dried jerky which Matt liked to carry in his pocket and munch. . . . Looking about the long room, Patricia desperately wanted her mother now. To advise with calm wisdom, to understand her slow steps to the door, and outside, to find Matt and tell him.

Men in the wide, busy ranch yard . . . Strange faces, strange names . . . Hammering, sawing . . . The musical, metallic ringing of the anvil in the small blacksmith shed . . . Some of the strange faces grinned at her as she passed. Rough, hard faces, many of whom she did not even know. Her smile was mechanical. "Where's Dad?"

Matt walked around the end of the bunkhouse. *Don't run.* She was smiling as she told Matt.

Matt said, "You don't say?" as if he heard this every morning. Then his creased face lighted with a great smile. He reached for her. His hug was a bear hug. "I've kinda hoped," Matt said. His rope-burned hand patted her shoulder. "Roger," Matt said, "gets you, an' I—"

"—get a son!" Patricia said with him, and her laughter came unrestrained from too much emotion too quickly.

They walked slowly across the yard.

"Ain't too important now, I guess," Matt said. "But while that young lawyer's here, I'm deedin' half of the ranch to

82

Roger. Rapburn's a notary. He'll record it in the courthouse at Socorro. You can sign for that share come to you from your mother." Matt's broad grin came again. "All of it in the family now for the next thirty years." His grin was anticipating. "Be kids around now. Half a dozen, maybe a dozen. Whoopin', playin'—a real family again."

In Patricia's trunk was a faded daguerreotype of Matt the year he was married, his face unlined, handsome. Young. Eager-looking, reckless-looking . . . Easy to believe any girl would have loved that young Matt Kilgore . . . And she had seen Matt sad and dispirited, gray and old-looking and beaten before Roger had come. Now a youthful eagerness was in Matt again. He was happy.

"Whoa, Grandfather!" Patricia said, laughing. "I'll sign whatever has to be signed. Then I'm going to ride out and calm this whirling head."

She rode north, quirting the horse into a muscle-bunching, lunging climb up the steep ridge slope through brush and trees, not minding slapping branches and the dangerous, dodging twists her horse made. Contrite, Patricia finally rested the sweating, blowing horse, and then rode on more slowly.

Familiar country. Sinuous, grassy draws flooded with sunlight, spotted with gay wildflowers. Ridges dark with trees and brush. In blue distance, the mountains serene and massive . . . All this her mother had loved. It was Matt's life. Roger had a feeling for it. Now Roger owned half. Thirty years from now, she and Roger . . .

Near midday Patricia was musing on the years ahead when a thought intruded and held her. Roger had not said that he loved her. Nor had she told Roger so. They had taken it for granted—and probably that was the way it usually was, Patricia guessed, smiling a little.

Nevertheless, the thought left a curious flatness that was still with her when she sighted the ranch buildings across the far, undulating sweep of the grass flats. She had ridden a great circle and was returning from the southeast.

Still thinking of Roger, Patricia listened idly to the soft, swishing scuff of the walking horse through the long grass, the rhythmic creak of saddle leather. The rider in distance across the flats was worth only a glance. Some man following the ranch road to the house, too far away to be recognized— Then, suddenly, all her scattered thoughts rushed together in a knot of foreboding.

That rider in distance ahead of her rode a black horse! He had a solitary, ominous look, sure of himself, as he deliberately, unhurriedly advanced toward the ranch yard.

14

Once Clay had tracked down a wounded and vicious grizzly which had killed a friend. That day his every move had been cautious, because the brute might have been waiting for him.

Today the same feeling went with him to the Kilgore ranch. Clay did not look over his shoulder at the sun-flooded grass flats running off into the southeast. If he had, he would have sighted the distant figure riding sidesaddle, and would have turned toward her, and the day might have been different.

In the Navajo-Ute country, old Ira Bell had said that Matt Kilgore owned a run-down ranch which Kilgore would probably soon lose. Ira Bell, Clay thought with alerting interest, should see this.

New structures had been built. New corrals were visible, some not finished. . . . Too many horses and men in sight for a working cattle ranch. One more man's arrival seemed to be ignored as the black gelding quickened toward a log watering trough in the ranch yard.

While the horse drank, Clay looked around. The house was low and wide, of thick-walled adobe, yellow-brown like the earth from which it had been built. Front and side *portals* had screening morning-glory and trumpet vines studded with bright flowers. The weathered earthen walls had the look of having been lived in a long time. Patricia Kilgore, Clay supposed, was inside the house. He put off meeting her and walked the black slowly back into the large yard, trying to guess which man was Travis.

A blacksmith's hammer and anvil clanged loudly in an open-front shed. On back, in a new breaking corral, a big dun stallion was fighting snub-rope and post. Half a dozen men watched, grinning, through the corral bars, some calling advice.

A high-sided freight wagon was being unloaded at a new storehouse. Great piles of newly cut fence posts lifted back of the yard. Rough-sawed lumber was stacked near the posts. Beyond were empty wagons. Old wagons. New wagons. His money, Clay guessed, had paid for all this. And when he thought of it, a black and destructive mood moved in.

Several men at the breaking corral gazed in mild curiosity as the black gelding walked near. A small, wiry man called, "Lookin' for someone?"

Inside the corral the dun stallion's hoofs were stamping, trampling the hard ground. Lather flecked the big horse, nostrils flared red through the lifting dust and the stallion's eyes rolled in a wild fury of protest. The same mood worked behind Clay's calm face as he put hands on the saddle horn and eyed the wiry man.

"Travis," Clay said. "Where's Roger Travis?"

"Been in the house all mornin'," was the idle reply.

A blocky looking man called roughly over a shoulder as he watched the stallion's lunges. "I been waitin' two hours fer Travis."

An older man passed the freight wagon and headed toward Clay with a look of authority. His vigorous shock of gray hair, and seamed face cut with lines of force and humor had a resemblance to Dick Kilgore. Clay put his horse toward the man and swung off.

"Matt Kilgore?" Because of Dick, warmth broke through despite Clay's mood.

"I'm Kilgore." The man was not big, but he seemed big in the way of a man who was big inside. And, close now, Clay noted shadings of sadness on the man's weathered face.

85

"I'm Clay Mara." Watchfully Clay wondered what would happen. Nothing happened.

"Howdy," said Matt Kilgore heartily. His brown vest open over heavy gunbelt, a thumb hooked behind the buckle of the belt, Kilgore stepped to the black. A square, rope-scarred hand shoved under the mane and flipped up the coarse black hairs, uncovering the neck brand. "How'd you get a saddle on one of my horses?" Kilgore asked calmly.

Clay's reply was laconic. "My horse now. Got a bill of sale for him." And, when Kilgore dropped the mane and turned back, Clay added, "From your daughter."

Matt Kilgore stared at him. "When'd Patricia start sellin' off horses?"

"Ask her and learn what's happening on your ranch."

"Wringy, ain't you?" said Kilgore after a moment. His head was cocked slightly and the shock of gray hair gave a youthful edge to the gusty force and drive which filled the man. The level regard had sharpened, cooled, as if Kilgore sensed the black currents in this stranger. "Patricia ain't here right now."

"Get Travis then."

"Roger's in the house talkin' with his lawyer, so's the fellow can start back to Socorro." Clay was the taller man. But Matt Kilgore, with the look of bigness and force, rocked on worn boot heels and ran a glance over the rangy hardness of the man before him. Kilgore's faint smile was approving. "Travis hire you in town yesterday an' fix you up with a horse?"

"Travis tried to see me."

Kilgore nodded. "Got use for a wringy one like you. If you an' Travis didn't settle it in town, we'll fix it now. Hire you myself."

Dark humor stirred in Clay at the idea of working alongside Travis, and the man unsuspecting. *If* Travis were unsuspecting. Slowly Clay pulled pipe and tobacco from his jacket pocket. "What kind of work?"

"What you're told to do."

Clay glanced about the yard. In the breaking corral, the stallion paused, wind whistling through flaring nostrils. The men were drifting away. The big fellow who had called irritably over a shoulder was turning a gray horse away from the corral. That gray horse prodded vaguely at Clay's memory as he answered Kilgore coolly.

"You aren't hiring to work cattle. You're hiring for trouble."

Kilgore was unruffled. "Been trouble before. Goes with the job."

Clay thumbed tobacco into the pipe, remembering what he'd heard in town. "Trouble with Gid Markham?" He watched a flinty look fill Kilgore's stare and harden, flatten in Kilgore's voice.

"I'll do all the guessin'. You hire here, you take what comes. I give orders!"

Evenly, Clay asked, "Who's got the money? Who pays me?"

It cut into Matt Kilgore's challenge, jerking a muscle at the corner of his mouth and holding him quiet while something like pain and sadness from deep memories clouded his look. Slowly Kilgore said, "Strangers pick up talk. Your tongue is sharp for it. I'll still hire you. But first I'll straighten you out. Travis is half-owner and marryin' my girl in a few days. But thirty years I been boss here. I'm still boss. That settle you?"

"Something to think about."

The slow steps of a horse coming up behind Clay hardly registered. He heard the nasal voice which had called over a shoulder at the breaking corral speak roughly behind him. "Kilgore, I done cooled heels too long. Tell Travis next time he leaves word for Grady Doyle to come in quick, he can be ready. Before I leave, I got to have some shells for my raafle."

Clay stood motionless while memories of the howling sandstorm and thirsty horse herd hit him. . . . He saw again the frantic try of the pinto horse for water, and the callous gunshot which had dropped the pinto. . . . *Raafle.*

Clay shoved the pipe into his jacket pocket, and asked Matt Kilgore evenly, "He your man?"

"Sounds so, don't he?"

Clay wheeled to the face he had seen masked by a bandanna through the sand clouds driving across the Red

87

Rock ledges. It was a broad face with a meaty look, recently cleaned by a razor. Eyebrows were a dark mat, and Clay recognized the gray horse now. It had been in Ira Bell's herd.

"So the name is Grady Doyle?" Clay said. "I carried the canteens at the Red Rocks!" And he thought, *Horsethieves. I come for Travis and find this.*

In startled shock, Doyle was reaching to the tied-down holster on his leg. And memories of what this man had done drove Clay into a silent leap, grabbing up for Doyle's thick gun wrist. His other hand slapped high into the blue bandanna folds around the muscular neck.

Doyle dropped the reins and struck wildly. The blow rocked Clay's head and flipped off his hat. The startled gray horse was whirling. Clay hung to the gun wrist and gouged fingers deep into the man's cording neck muscles.

Bracing against the furious kick of Doyle's foot in the stirrup, Clay man-handled the man over and out of the saddle. Someone yelled joyously, "Fight startin'!" as Clay wrestled the burly body half under him.

They slammed with shock to the ground between the horses. The half-drawn gun jolted out of the holster as they thrashed in the dirt. Clay forced Doyle's straining hand away from the gun. His thumb drove deep into Doyle's windpipe.

Doyle beat wildly at Clay's face. Livid, as his wind was cut off, Doyle frantically twisted over against a leg of the gray horse. Clay let go and lunged up to his feet, sucking deep breaths. His kick drove Doyle's gun skittering out of reach.

Matt Kilgore's bawled order lifted. "Git that gray hoss outa the way!" Kilgore was wheeling the black gelding away.

Clay sighted a blur of men running in. He could have used a gun as Doyle scrambled up almost under the gray horse's belly. And Doyle's friends would finish Clay Mara—and Travis would have the years ahead. The thought loosed all the wildness Clay had kept locked in. As Doyle came upright, hatless and gasping, Clay jumped in silence again.

Doyle tried to dodge. Clay's looping fist smashed Doyle's

88

mouth, spinning the man floundering around to hands and knees again.

Matt Kilgore shouted, "Let 'em finish, long as a gun ain't pulled!"

At the moment, Doyle seemed the only one who knew what the trouble was about. *Silence* him, and there was a chance, then, to break out of the circle of armed men. Doyle's lips were torn and bleeding as he bounced up and circled away. He spat red and his eyes watched the holstered gun under Clay's jacket.

Clay pitched his revolver away before Doyle could grab for it, and Doyle ran at him, ducking, striking furiously. Clay jumped aside. His jolting blow gouged across Doyle's cheek. Doyle wheeled fast, diving at him and reaching out. Clay dodged too slowly and Doyle's big hand caught the front of his canvas jacket and pulled him close.

A hard uppercut struck Doyle's solid jaw. Doyle threw his other arm around Clay's neck and let go of the jacket. His fist punched shocking blows to Clay's ribs. The man's burly power was now evident. His gasping breaths snorted and blew against Clay's neck.

Dimly Clay heard a spectator whoop. "This gets him!"

Clay threw himself back, dragging Doyle. He twisted inside the clamping arm, kicked behind Doyle's foot and tripped the man. And got hands down and broke his own fall. A tremendous twist, a roll, and Clay wrenched his head out of the viselike arm, rolled again and drove up away from Doyle's grabbing hand. Half-sick from one great blow to the middle, Clay heard the jeer of his own thoughts: *Travis wins.*

Doyle was scrambling up after him, mouth smeared red and swelling, eyes glaring. And the thought of Travis filled Clay, corrosive and compelling. He met Doyle with a great blow to the mouth. Doyle stopped short, shuddering, shaking his head, blowing out mashed lips. Clay jumped in and struck terribly under the ribs. Doyle's hands came down and Clay belted the heavy jaw.

Doyle's hands came up in a shocked, instinctive gesture. And Clay rolled wide shoulders and grunted as he drove a

89

fist in above Doyle's belt, sinking it deep. Doyle backed away, bending helplessly, gulping for breath that would not come, and Clay followed him. The long fury was driving him now to beat this burly stranger down, and get at Travis and the Kilgores. Rolling his shoulders, crouching a little, Clay drove fists into Doyle's face.

And as Doyle went back, uncertainty bloomed muddy and dull in Doyle's eyes. He was sensing a new ferocity as Clay leaped on top of him.

Silence had dropped on the watching men. Only harsh, sucking breaths and the sodden sounds of Clay's fists were audible. Doyle's head rocked and bobbed. His burly frame shuddered as slashing knuckles tore his face into a travesty, and his confidence visibly drained away.

Clay thought of Howie Quist. Doyle's face swelling and smeared would stir Howie's humor. Clay grinned at the thought. And his humor at a time like this shocked Doyle. It was visible.

Clay's arms were weary. His lungs felt on fire. But the thought of Howie's satisfaction kept the humor on his face as he reached out to Doyle's coat and dragged the big man close, and struck the great blob of a face with measured calculation.

That almost leisurely blow of complete ferocity, with humor visible behind it, crumpled Doyle inside. He quit; it was in his eyes and the sudden slackness of face and body.

Clay held him by the coat and heard, far away it seemed, a harsh question. "Who's that fellow beating Doyle?"

Sounding far away through their sobbing breaths, Kilgore's reply was audible. "Name's Clay Mara. I thought you knowed him, Roger." Then Kilgore's irritated protest, "Let 'em alone!"

A vicious blow above Clay's ear drove him into Doyle and they fell together.

15

When Patricia Kilgore rode fast into the big ranch yard behind the house, she saw the crew bunched together in excitement. The men parted for her blowing horse, and Patricia saw a revolver in Roger Travis's hand, and two inert figures on the ground.

Matt called to her, "Wait in the house, Patricia! This ain't for you!"

Patricia reached for a lifted hand and dropped off the sidesaddle, and tightly asked, "Did you have to kill him?"

The stranger named Clay Mara sprawled on the ground, his cheek in the dirt. And Roger's reply held anger which Patricia had never heard from him. "I clubbed the fellow off of Doyle!"

Patricia swallowed as she looked at the man who must be Doyle. He was trying to get up. Braced on big, splayed hands and knees, Doyle swayed dazedly. . . . Like a helpless bear, Patricia thought, appalled. A big, battered bear of a man covered with dust and dirt. His head sagged and wobbled. One eye was swelling shut. His battered, puffy face peered blindly around as Matt's brusque voice corrected Roger.

"They was settlin' something and Roger butted in. I told him to keep out."

Roger had never talked to Matt as he did now, angry and coldly ironic. "When did you start feeling sorry for Gid Markham's roughnecks, Matt?"

"I never did!"

"You're looking at one! That stranger Mara!"

Matt's startled glance sought Patricia.

"That right?" Matt's hardening voice demanded, and when Patricia nodded, Matt's harshness drove at her. "How come he got a horse from you?"

Patricia looked at the listening men. "I'll explain, Dad."

"You sure will! Right here, quick!"

"In the house."

"All I want—is he a Markham man you had truck with?"

Patricia felt her swift flush. "In the house, Dad!" she repeated.

Matt snapped to the nearest men, "Lug him to the house!" and stalked away.

Roger caught Doyle's arm and dragged the burly man to his feet. Patricia had an uncertain thought that she could almost be afraid of Roger when he looked like this.

Four men hoisted the stranger by legs and arms and carried his sagging body toward the house. Mechanically Patricia picked up his trampled old gray hat and the revolver near it. Behind her, Jim Rapburn said, "Anything I can do?"

Rapburn's expensive gray suit, white linen, polished shoes, and the hat politely in his hand, belonged to the towns, not this empty, wild country which was her life and Matt's life, and into which Roger had fitted easily. Even the stranger, Clay Mara, was like the booted, armed crew and the violence which had erupted here. But not this young lawyer with his sensitive face flushed now with excitement.

"It's finished," said Patricia as calmly as she could. . . . And she knew it wasn't finished. Clay Mara was a threatening beginning. Doyle was a part of it. And, in the background, was Gid Markham now. All her life the Markhams had been in the background.

Rapburn's comment held admiration. "Travis is quite a man, isn't he?"

Patricia watched Roger Travis propel the stumbling Doyle back in the yard.

"Roger," she said, absently, "did what he thought best, I suppose.". . . *Roger had struck Clay Mara down from behind. Mara would not forget.*

Patricia's smile at the lawyer was forced as she left him there and walked toward the house, and found herself thinking of the *padre's* quiet voice explaining the age-old meanings of Amos, Gideon and Matthew.

Amos Markham was dead.

But, suddenly now, Amos Markham was very real again,

that dour, cold man who had known his Bible—Amos, "bearer of a burden.". . . And the son he had named Gideon, "the hewer-down"—the destroyer—was alive and ominous. And Gid Markham's gunman—this man Clay Mara—was in the house now, possessing knowledge which would drive Gid Markham into fierce retaliation against the Kilgores. Patricia carried that shaken thought into the house.

Grady Doyle mumbled dazed threats as Travis guided his lurching steps toward the back of the yard.

"Shut up!" Travis said. He shoved the arm he gripped and Doyle staggered. The anger Travis was restraining because curious eyes were watching drew his words into thin bitterness. "This man Mara walked in, bringing a wounded man and that sorrel horse I turned over to you. What was the trouble?" And, when Doyle remained silent, Travis spoke with full viciousness, "I'll finish what he started and get the story from you anyway!"

Doyle groaned. "How'd he know me? He never seen my face!"

They reached the empty wagons beyond the piles of new fence posts and lumber. A final shove sent Doyle stumbling against a wagon wheel. "Now tell it!" ordered Travis coldly.

Doyle clutched the wheel rim. His left eye was swelling shut, so that he peered with a lopsided squint from the other eye. "A drifter come through Soledad," Doyle mumbled, sullenly. "He'd talked to an old man in the Navajo country who was tradin' for hosses and fixin' to come south by the Red Rocks."

"I see," said Travis, almost gently. "A little horse stealing on the side. Well, go on."

Doyle's story came out in disjointed, sullen bits. "Markham horses!" Travis said so softly and violently that Doyle flinched. "Six of you holed up, waiting, with the horse herd sighted through glasses before the sandstorm hit. And you let all three Markham men get away to tell it!"

"Sand was blowin' fearful," Doyle muttered.

Travis walked slowly to the front of the wagon. He had known trouble was breaking when he had emerged from the house and found Grady Doyle being mauled by the stranger

93

named Mara. He had ignored Matt Kilgore's order to let the two men alone. Questioning Doyle quickly had been more important. But he would not have believed it could be as bad as this. He stood for some moments trying to guess what would happen now, and shifting his own plans to meet it.

When Travis turned back, Doyle sullenly said, "Wasn't no way of knowin' they was Markham hosses 'til the old man yelled it."

Travis gave Doyle another malevolent look.

"You let this man Mara raid your camp, slash your saddles, take your horses and bridles and canteens—and then find you here at the ranch!" And, because anger was no help now, Travis forced calm and ordered, "Wait here. I'll be back."

Young Jim Rapburn was sitting uncertainly in his livery buggy, ready to leave.

"You can start back, Jim." Travis was calm because he had made many decisions as he crossed the big yard. "Don't wait in Soledad for the Socorro stage. Hire a buckboard and driver from the stageline and use their relay teams to get through as fast as possible. Get that deed to half this ranch recorded in the courthouse at once. And start everything else quickly."

Rapburn's thin face sobered. "Is it that bad?"

"Gid Markham will make trouble now. I'll move before he can." And, because he was sure of young Rapburn now, Travis spoke with conviction he tried to feel himself. "With Markham pushed out of this country, I'll be so solidly set I can handle anything else that happens. But it must be done fast now."

Rapburn hesitated. Caution filled his question. "Will Matt Kilgore support every move? He hasn't been told everything, you know—and this is his ranch."

"Half Matt's ranch now," reminded Travis brusquely. "The moment you get that deed recorded, my word carries as much authority here as Matt's. I'll handle Matt. And, Jim?"

"Yes?"

94

"You're my lawyer, not Matt's lawyer. My interests come first."

"Of course." Rapburn had another thought. "Shall I retain the other three lawyers in Socorro for you?"

"Tie 'em up," Travis decided. He stood by the buggy, estimating the young lawyer. "One more thing, Jim. Perhaps the most important. I want you to put out feelers in Socorro for any strangers who might ask questions about me or the Kilgores or this ranch. Any sort of curiosity at all."

Puzzled, Rapburn said, "Strangers?"

"Anyone you or your friends don't personally know. If you hear of any such curious person, get word to me as fast as possible."

"It would be someone connected with Gid Markham, I suppose?"

"The man wouldn't admit it." Travis eyed the slight flush of excitement which had come on young Rapburn's sensitive face. His warming smile came. "Jim, have you decided what you'll be one of these days? The Delegate to Congress? Or a judge? Or merely the leading lawyer in the Territory?"

Rapburn's smile came too as he visualized again the rich future Travis was boldly driving for now.

"I'll not have any trouble deciding when the time comes," Rapburn said. The smile was still on his face as he drove off on the long, fast trip back to Socorro.

Travis's smile faded as the grinding tension tightened inside once more. . . . *How much time did he have before the real Roger Travis appeared?*

Last night, alone in his quiet bedroom, he had read again in the journal kept by the man, and the real Roger Travis had come alive with sweating clarity—taking the form of the stranger who had tried to draw money from the Travis account in the South Bay Bank in San Francisco. Travis had not slept well. And Grady Doyle's sullen confession just now had deepened the uneasy feeling that luck might be turning against him.

His luck wasn't turning, Travis knew. A man made his own luck, as he was making it now. Digging in swiftly, until no stranger with a fantastic story could dislodge him—or live long while trying.

On his way back across the yard, Travis picked up Grady Doyle's revolver and hat and caught the reins of Doyle's gray horse standing near by. He ran an estimating eye over the crew loitering around the yard still talking about the fight. They were tough men. They were ready and tired of waiting—and they would not wait long now.

Doyle had steadied when Travis got back to him. "Where are your men?" Travis coldly demanded.

Doyle punched out the trampled hat. "They got a lick of water into the old man's hosses an' run 'em on southwest. Joe an' me rode this way an' split up, lookin' for them three men."

"Joe," Travis made a biting guess, "must have found them. He won't be back." He considered Doyle. "I can still use you." Doyle started to grin, and Travis added with abrupt viciousness again, "But you'll take orders!"

Doyle's kind understood such talk; his lopsided squint peered as he agreed, "I ain't arguin'. What's orders?"

"Ride the country and look for any stranger who shows interest in the Kilgores or me. If he smokes a straight-stemmed pipe, get word to me fast."

Doyle's puffy mouth grinned. "That oughta be easy."

"If you spot the right man," said Travis evenly, "he's worth two hundred dollars to you."

Doyle's puffy grin lingered. "Want 'im killed?"

"I'm not telling you to." And, because he knew Doyle's kind, Travis warned coldly, "Don't put a pipe in a dead man's pocket. I'll know!"

Grady Doyle did not glance back as he rode away. And it occurred to Travis that young Chet Davis, who was watching the Markham ranch, could watch for strangers also. And all the large crew here could watch.

Dark amusement briefly pushed back the tension as Travis thought how the money of the real Roger Travis was shaping a trap for the fellow.

Then the bronzed stranger in the house, the man named Clay Mara who rode for Gid Markham, took over Travis's immediate thinking. Mara, too, could be handled with

96

money. All men could. And Mara could be used. What was coming quickly now against Gid Markham would be violent and ruthless, Travis knew. Thinking about it in hardening purpose, Travis walked to the house.

16

The men had dropped Clay Mara on the wide, worn planks of the kitchen floor like a dead man. Only he wasn't a dead man, Patricia knew with antagonism as she tossed his dusty hat and revolver on the checked tablecloth. Men laid out with a gun barrel were quickly as dangerous as ever.

Without sympathy, Patricia located a slow, steady pulse in his muscular wrist. Yard dirt covered his dark wool pants and canvas jacket, and smeared his face. Red, raw scratches reached across his strong jaw. With a damp towel from the sink, Patricia wiped his face impersonally, like a piece of furniture. She used the towel to slap dirt off his clothes.

His bronzed face, shaved smooth today, looked younger. Deceptively harmless, helpless, peaceful. A purplish, swollen bruise on the side of his head marked where Roger's gun barrel had struck him down. Patricia coolly examined the spot and let it alone. A leather sheath on his hip held a long keen knife. She took the knife. A slight bulge in the front of his shirt was a second revolver. . . . *A tricky man, ready for trouble.* . . . An object in the pocket of his brush jacket was not the small gun Patricia expected. Her hand brought out a reeking, straight-stemmed pipe.

Patricia's greenish blue, resentful eyes looked at the pipe. Matt always said that a pipe smoker was steady and dependable. *Wrong on this stranger.* Patricia tossed the pipe, revolver, and knife on the table beside his old hat. A moment later Matt's worn boot heels thumped into the kitchen with a vigorous sound of purpose.

Matt's seamed face was grim under his youthful shock of gray hair. He scooped her into a hug, wiping out his temper in the yard, and then bent over the man.

"Now," Matt said, "what about that black hoss you sold him?"

"Two days ago, Dad, he came walking in to the Soledad road, leading a sorrel horse—"

Matt rocked on his boot heels and listened intently. With his vest sagging open, thumb hooked on the wide, cartridge-studded gunbelt, he had the old look of solid force which had been the shield and strength of the family through so many years. And Matt's irrepressible humor, back also these days, found a grin in her account of the black gelding substituted for the sorrel.

"You made a try," Matt said. "All anyone c'n do." He looked at the stranger on the floor and said slowly, "That Doyle that Roger hired is mixed in it."

"You hired Doyle," Patricia reminded.

"Never seen him before," Matt said flatly. "Wouldn'ta hired him if I had. Don't like his looks."

"Roger said—"

Matt flicked her an odd look. "Roger said I hired Doyle?"

"I probably misunderstood—" Anything which made Roger seem less than perfect to Matt could be pushed aside. Like sweeping stray dirt under the carpet, Patricia's guilty thought came.

Matt's odd, level look stayed on her face for a moment. "You heerd wrong," said Matt calmly. "Doyle rode in saying he worked for Roger, an' Roger wanted to see him."

Roger had lied about Doyle in Soledad. Why? Patricia tried not to think so. But she remembered clearly.

Matt was studying the stranger on the floor. "This feller," Matt said, "knowed who Doyle was when Doyle rode up behind him. This one turned and said, 'I carried the canteens at the Red Rocks!' An' Doyle grabbed for his gun."

Startled, Patricia said, "This man didn't start it?"

"Nope," said Matt, "but he sure finished it. He jumped like a broom-busted pup and dragged Doyle off the hoss." A glint in Matt's eye made clear the sight had stirred and delighted him. Matt reached for one of the revolvers on the table and examined it. "He packin' two guns?"

"That gun was inside his shirt." Patricia could not resist a barbed, "Look at his pipe. What do you think of a pipe smoker now?"

Matt's eyes twinkled at her. "Same thing I always did. Means a steady man."

"This man steady?" Patricia was scornful.

Matt's wry smile came. "You ain't learned much about men, honey. He had two guns an' he didn't even use one. He coulda blowed that Doyle off the hoss, but he dragged the big loudmouth off an' used his hands."

"He was brutal!"

"He was a pure pleasure to watch," said Matt, and his grin spread at the memory. "Fast as a cat. After he got goin', he tore the feller apart. It was a sight."

"You sound as bad as he is!"

Matt chuckled. "I've tore a few apart myself when I was a young rooster. Got tore, too." Soberness returned as Matt laid the gun back on the table. "Plain enough now there was a big hassle out at the Red Rock Tanks. Doyle an' this one was in it, an' Mara caught Doyle here." Matt's voice hardened. "An' I mean to hear why any man that Roger hired was swappin' shots away out there at the Red Rocks with Markham men." Matt's thumb jerked at the table. "Get Mara's truck out of reach before he gets on his feet and we got a hassle here in the house. He won't feel kindly, an' he ain't a feller to fool with."

Patricia was dropping the stranger's possessions into a drawer by the sink when Roger walked in and casually inquired, "How is he?"

Matt was cool. "He was doing all right, son, 'til you butted in."

Patricia had heard that deliberate edge in Matt's voice before. All her brothers had heard it—and always apprehensively. When Matt sounded like that he was about to crack down, sternly, relentlessly. . . . *But to Roger?*

Roger was indifferent. "I did what I thought best."

"Like hirin' that feller Doyle an' givin' him a horse?"

"If you put it that way, Matt."

99

"I've just started puttin' it," said Matt's deliberate voice. "You been talkin' to Doyle. What happened out at the Red Rocks?"

Roger's shrug held regret. "Matt, I hired the wrong man, it seems. Doyle knew this man would tell everything, so Doyle admitted that he rode out on his own with some men and stole some horses."

"At the Red Rocks?"

"Yes."

Matt's level guess came. "Markham hosses."

"It seems so."

"And a Markham man was shot," said Matt evenly.

"Not killed."

Matt looked bigger, suddenly, than Roger—big, fierce and stern. "You got any idea what a mess you've made?"

Roger said the wrong thing, hardening. "Look, Matt, I'm not a kid. Don't talk to me like I am!"

Coldly Matt said, "You'll get it from me like one of my own boys'd get it. You're in the family now. It's time you learned. We never took a step back from the Markhams."

"We won't now, Matt!"

"I'm talkin'! You listen! Amos Markham was a mean one. He raised Gid the same way when it come to us. But Amos an' Gid always knew—an' we knew, too—nobody'd get shot in the back. We all knew there'd be no stock rustled. The Markhams kep' pride. I'll give 'em that. An' never a day a Kilgore couldn't give 'em the same!"

Patricia understood all the great, fierce bitterness which filled Matt's tone.

"Thirty years!" Matt said. "An' *now* a Markham can call us horsethieves—an' this feller on the floor can make it stick!"

Roger's long-boned face was hardening in anger and resentment when Patricia quickly warned, "This man's eyes are open. He's listening."

Through hot flickers of pain, Clay had heard, first, Matt Kilgore's jarring boot heels entering the room. Motionless, while haze cleared from his mind, Clay had listened. And in brief minutes he had come to know the Kilgores as they were. . . . After Patricia's sharp warning, hostile silence fell.

With gritting effort, Clay sat up. Pain jumped in his head as he braced with a hand on the floor. His guns had been taken. His back-brushing arm found the sheath knife gone. And Travis was armed.

Matt Kilgore brusquely warned as Clay got to a knee and unsteadily to his feet, "Easy, Mara! I got enough trouble now to settle!"

"Think you can settle it?" Clay asked sourly. He spoke to Patricia. "Where's my sorrel horse?"

She faced him, her black, piled hair no more than shoulder high to him, and greenish blue eyes direct and antagonistic. "I gave you a better horse."

Pretty. Full of spirit, Clay thought. Maliciously he said, "Your business if you go around giving horses to strangers. I still want my sorrel." Clay turned his tightening stare to Travis. His hand lifted to his head where the man's gun barrel had slashed in. "You dropped me from behind!" Clay said with such low threat that it tightened Travis's long-angled, handsome features.

Travis's hand loosed a coat button and the coat opened over his shell belt and gun. "So what?" Travis said so viciously that Patricia's startled look flashed to him.

"Let be, you two! I'll talk," Matt Kilgore said grimly. "Pay heed, Mara! Roger figured a Markham man was beating one of our crew an' jumped in to help."

Clay's retort was caustic. "I heard you try to stop him. Who's boss on this ranch?"

Kilgore's rope-scarred hand gestured impatiently. "No matter now. You laid on the floor hearing we had no thought that Doyle was stealin' hosses. Let alone Markham hosses."

"Gid Markham didn't hear it," said Clay shortly. He was eyeing Travis, trying to judge the man's intent.

From the floor the fellow had looked tall, wide-shouldered, aggressive, sure of himself in the expensive blue suit. *My money bought that suit,* Clay's acid thought came.

Travis was measuring him with a flinty, calculating look. *Tough,* Clay judged. He knew the type, he'd met many such. This sort of man would try anything. . . . Clay's hard, braced wariness tried to guess, *Does he know me?*

They were watching each other with hard alertness when Matt Kilgore made another impatient gesture. "Gid Markham will hear it from Doyle's own mouth, young feller, before you can run to Markham with the story!" The fierceness and bitterness of moments ago had become heavy, forceful calm in Kilgore.

Travis pulled a cigar from the breast pocket of his blue coat and frowned as he jerked a match into flame under the table edge. When the cigar was going, Travis bent the match absently between his fingers and said coolly, "Matt, I fired Doyle and ran him off."

Matt Kilgore's soft *"God'lmighty!"* was fierce in its restraint. Kilgore's creased face went stony as he walked to the warm range, caught a white mug off a shelf, and reached for the big pot on the back of the stove. His voice was heavy. "Get coffee, Mara. You need it, too."

Dismay was plain on Patricia Kilgore's oval face. It filled her question to Travis. *"Why,* Roger? How can we explain that?"

Cynically Clay watched Travis's expression warm indulgently.

"Doyle," Travis said, smiling now, "wasn't a fool, Pat. He'd have sworn we sent him after those horses—and who would Markham have believed?"

Matt Kilgore, pouring coffee, said bluntly, "Gid'd believe Doyle, because he'd want to!"

"Doyle's gone," Travis said, still smiling. "Mara here is the only one who knows about Doyle now. And I'd rather have Mara with us, if he'll believe I made a mistake about him and can be friendly. I came in here to hire him, Matt. He's a better man than any we've got. We need him."

"Tried to hire 'im myself," Matt admitted.

Mildly, Travis said, "Mara, how about it?"

Kilgore went motionless, mug in hand. Clay saw Patricia's greenish blue, direct eyes fixed on him with something like bated hope.

"Friendly?" Clay said. "Working for you?" The humor of it bent Clay's mouth in a grin as he took a swallow of coffee from the mug he held. "Miss Kilgore might object. She owes me a sorrel horse I mean to collect."

102

Patricia bit her lip. She was a striking girl, Clay thought now, slender, alert as she gazed directly at him, flushing slightly. Coolly she said, "You can have the sorrel."

"Want me to work here, ma'am?"

"I have nothing to do with it."

"I come high when I work."

Travis said, "Name it."

"I hear in town you've got plenty of money," Clay said, the humor still in him at thought of working for this man and being paid with his own money.

Travis said easily, "I've got enough money."

Clay chuckled across the coffee mug he was lifting. "Wrong, fellow. You haven't got enough to cover turning a horsethief loose so you can duck blame." Clay's grin widened as he took another swallow of coffee and watched Travis's smile cut off in a flare of anger.

Matt Kilgore's harsh *Enough!* abruptly dominated the big kitchen. Kilgore set his mug on the range, jarring hard and slopping coffee. "Mara! Get jerky off the wall to chew if you're hungry. I'll take you back safe to Gid Markham, so's anything might happen to you won't be on us. Let's go!"

Patricia objected apprehensively, "Dad! There's no way you can reason with Gid Markham!"

Flat and harsh Kilgore said, "Got to be done. I'm head of the family. My place to do it. No talk now! We're startin'!"

Kilgore's black hat was pulled low as he rode with Clay on the ranch road across the wide flats, and to the right, up through thickening brush and cedar scrub. Lines had creased deeper in the man's face. His silence had a grim, withdrawn quality.

"We're short-cuttin'," said Kilgore finally. "Be rough ridin'."

He was Dick Kilgore's father—this broad-chested, gray-haired man riding straight-up, the buffetings of the past driven deep into his leathery face in strength and sadness. A fair man, with inflexible inner strength, Clay knew now. Back at the house, Travis had tried to argue, and Kilgore had cut him off with solid purpose, which still did not hide strong affection for Travis.

The jarring pain in Clay's head was easing when they blew

the horses on the ridge crest. Looking back and down, Clay's gaze sharpened on a buggy stringing pale dust along the road ruts they had left.

"Looks like Mrs. Strance's buggy," Clay said. "The widow who owns the newspaper."

Kilgore looked and nodded. "Dot Strance comes out to see Patricia now'n then."

Clay gave a last hard look back at the distant buggy as they rode on. The woman's questions about San Francisco still troubled him. The widow must have left Soledad shortly after he had—and she was driving straight to Travis. She meant, evidently, to make trouble for Clay Mara.

They were crossing a mile-wide valley of open grass toward a high mesa rim when Kilgore said, "Long time ago I busted acrost here with four young Apache bucks quirtin' behind, sure they had me cornered against that mesa rise ahead."

Clay scanned the valley. "I'd have been sure of you, too."

Kilgore smiled faintly. "There's a washed cut in that wall ahead. I got my hoss up it, bellied on the rim up there, an' put them young bucks afoot. Couple years later one of their old men told me they was a sheepish bunch after they walked clean back to the wickiups on Big Jack Mountain."

Dark memories of Wyoming hit Clay. "Might have been your family next time, and those four doing it."

" 'Twould of been my family sure enough if I'd kilt 'em," said Kilgore quietly. "Twicet, anyway, it was my family. One of my boys each time."

"And you stayed on in the country," said Clay under his breath.

Quietly Kilgore said, "Two hundred years it's been happening in this New Mexico country. This was home. Blood in the ground for payment." Kilgore's wry smile came. "The old men in the Rio Grande settlements say the Indians— Utes an' Navajos, Apaches, Comanches—always left enough for a new start. Enough women to raise more women. Sheep, cattle, hosses to start over. That way the raiding stayed good."

"It has a sound," Clay said, "of the settlements being kept like chickens for plucking."

"The chickens plucked back. They was always Indian slaves on the haciendas an' in the settlements. Which is why they's so many dark skins an' broad cheekbones roundabout. Lot of mixing has gone on in two hundred years of fightin' and raidin' in this country."

"Did they ever clean you?" Clay inquired curiously.

Kilgore nodded. "I never quite made it back after the last cleanin'. Took Roger Travis to do it. He was my last boy's partner. We're makin' a new start now."

The cliff loomed above them, as it had to Matt Kilgore long ago in his furious ride for life. This time their horses crunched leisurely over a fan of dry sand and gravel and angled to the right into a narrow cut which gouged back and up. Kilgore led the way, his horse clashing, slipping, haunches bunching, straining as it drove up.

When Clay broke out at the top, Kilgore was adjusting cinches on his sweating horse.

"That day I come up twicet as fast," Kilgore called. And, when Clay stepped down beside him, Kilgore held out Clay's two revolvers and sheath knife he had been carrying. "Couldn't give 'em to you at the house, the way you looked at Roger," he said dryly.

"How did I look?"

"Your boss, Gid Markham is hotheaded. You ain't. Don't want you around Roger with a gun." Kilgore's faint smile considered Clay. "Myself, I kinda fancy you."

Clay shoved the heavy revolver back into the holster. His own slow smile came. "I was thinking the same thing about you," Clay said. When he turned to the black gelding to tighten cinches also, he heard Matt Kilgore's small chuckle. Moments later Clay reached into his jacket pocket. Then felt in other pockets.

"I had a pipe—"

"I mind it," Kilgore recalled, "on the table with that stuff Patricia took offen you. It went in that drawer I opened to get your guns. I clean forgot it."

"Leave it at the doctor's house next trip someone makes to town," Clay said. He had papers and rolled a smoke before they rode on across the broad, rising mesa flecked with green junipers like fat Christmas trees.

105

They reached tall, straight pines, and a small wind, cool at this higher altitude, tangy with conifer scent, soughed softly through the branches. A buck deer raced away through the trees in bounding leaps, its white flag bobbing erratically. They crossed a high meadow and, abruptly, they were descending over rough benches, down steep slopes, dropping off limestone ledges and skirting bald, massive outcroppings.

Kilgore spoke without visible emotion. "We're on Markham land."

Clay made no comment. He was wondering what had brought the red-haired, young Mrs. Strance so hastily to the Kilgore ranch. And how much she threatened his plans now.

17

When Patricia Kilgore glanced out the kitchen window and saw the dusty old pole buggy rolling into the yard behind the house, she hurried out with mixed emotions, reluctant to come under the scrutiny of Dot Strance's intelligent hazel eyes. Dot was a friend, but too much had just happened.

Dot was gazing from the buggy seat at empty wagons being moved to the high stacks of new-cut fence posts. Dull thuds of heavy posts being tossed into the wagons echoed through the brilliant sunlight. Cheerfully Dot inquired, "Cord wood?"

"Fence posts," said Patricia, and saw Roger Travis coming to them with long strides.

Casually Dot said, "I'm driving through to Piedras, and I thought you'd be interested to know that stranger, Clay Mara, came to me this morning asking about his sorrel horse."

"I played a trick on him," Patricia said guardedly, and guessed, "you drove out here to hear why I did." She was not resentful, but increasingly guarded. "Come in, Dot. Coffee's hot, and almost time to eat."

Dot Strance laughed.

"I *am* going on to Piedras, Pat. Well—one cup; then I'll have to get on."

Roger joined them. Hat in hand, smiling broadly, he helped Dot off the buggy step. Despite her usual plain outfit, Dot Strance looked lovely and young in a ripe, mature way, Patricia realized with vague envy. She felt immature beside the young widow.

Dot was composed and politely friendly to Roger. "Fencing land, Mr. Travis?"

"Here and there," said Roger carelessly. He stepped over and slipped an arm around Patricia. "You're in time for an announcement."

Dot Strance surveyed them, smiling. "Not too much of a surprise. Pat, I'm so happy for you."

Laughing, talking, they walked into the house. Patricia served coffee in her best willowware cups and, while she did so, her thoughts shadowed at the memory of Clay Mara's dark face coldly watching Roger. The grimness of Matt Kilgore's purpose as he started for the Markham ranch with Mara made it worse.

Dot stirred sugar into her coffee and spoke good-naturedly to Roger. "Were Patricia and her father amused by that clipping from the San Francisco newspaper?"

Roger shrugged ruefully. "I lost the clipping and forgot to mention it."

Patricia said, "Clipping from a San Francisco newspaper?"

Dot said lightly, "I thought the story might be about your Roger Travis, and I had intended to print it. Some stranger in San Francisco tried to draw money from the bank account of a man named R. Travis. When they tried to hold the man, he bluffed them with a pipestem in his coat pocket, and took the cashier with him when he walked out and drove away in a waiting carriage."

Carefully Patricia said, "A straight-stemmed pipe?" Her hand clenched under the table edge and she said the first thing that came to mind. "He wouldn't have had much chance if shooting had started."

"I think that man would have had a chance," said Dot with smiling conviction. "The bank cashier discovered it was

107

a pipe and leaped from the carriage. The coachman whipped up the horses and made a reckless escape through the city streets." Dot's smile lingered. "Unfortunately it wasn't our Mr. Travis's account. He's never been in San Francisco, or California, either."

Roger chuckled. "I still hope to get to California."

Dot Strance finished her coffee and suggested as she stood up, "A trip to California would be a nice honeymoon."

"One day Pat and I will get there," Roger said. "Just now we don't have the time."

Patricia stood up thinking with shock of the straight-stemmed pipe she had taken from the pocket of Mara's dusty canvas jacket. And, as she walked outside with Dot Strance and Roger, Patricia's glance went in almost frightened fascination to the drawer where she had dropped the pipe. . . . The front wheel of Dot's buggy cramped around, scraping briefly on the sharp turn. From the sagging seat, Dot waved as she drove away.

Roger stared after the buggy, his smile gone now. "I don't like her," he said shortly. "After we're married, we won't see much of her."

"That," Patricia said as she turned back into the house, "will take care of itself."

She knew Roger was staring at her back. She could visualize his long, strong face stiff and uncompromising as he walked back to the working men. And, blindly now, not looking at the drawer, Patricia walked through the kitchen to her bedroom, and closed the door.

Tucked away in the bottom of her small leather trunk studded with brass, was a packet of mementoes she would always cherish. One, in particular, was the last letter her brother Dick had written her from Central. America.

Patricia's hand was unsteady as she brought out the packet and sat on the edge of her bed and, slowly, with sick foreboding untied the faded pink ribbon around the packet. She found the letter with its odd-looking foreign stamp, and forced herself to read the contents and make certain her memory was correct about what Dick had written her. If her memory should be right . . . Patricia shivered.

108

Clay Mara was thinking with foreboding of the young widow Strance as Matt Kilgore led the way down into lower country, through draws filled with tall grass and scattered cattle. And, as they emerged from the maze of twisting finger draws into a small valley, Kilgore said, "Nigh there." The Markham headquarters was up the valley, an oasis marked by immense gray-green cottonwoods. "Mostly new since I seen it last," Kilgore commented.

Kilgore was riding at a steady, jolting trot, back straight, no expression at all on his creased face. One could only guess at the emotions roiling in the gray-haired impassive man.

The main house, Clay saw, was long and low, of tawny mud-plastered adobe. There was a small stream a horse could leap. Threadlike *acequia* channels carried water to garden and orchard. Corrals were of gnarled cedar trunks upright in the ground. Outbuildings behind the house were constructed in the form of a square, with high, thick adobe walls between them, so that the square formed by house, outbuildings and connecting walls enclosed a large yard. A gate of logs, open now, made house, yard and outbuildings a fort when closed.

Men were outside and inside the walled yard, with bread and meat and tin cups of coffee. A few moved about stiffly. Others, cross-legged on the ground as they ate, were taking their first rest, Clay judged, in a punishing day and night.

"Markham rode to the Red Rocks," Clay said. "Just back, by the looks."

Kilgore said, "You didn't let on." His impassiveness did not change.

Man after man stared incredulously as Kilgore's straight figure was recognized. One man swung around and bolted through the open gate into the yard in a half-run, coffee visibly slopping from the tin cup in his hand. Others stood up.

Kilgore showed no emotion over the stir his arrival was causing. Reins held casually in one hand, he pointed the steady trot of his horse to the waiting men.

The wiry figure of Gid Markham, still wearing the sober black suit, gray with dust now, bolted out of the back of the house. Unshaven, as exhausted looking as his crew, Markham stalked out of the gate. Kilgore reined down to a walk, then a halt, and Clay did the same as Markham met them.

Dust and grime were ground into the rough black stubble on Markham's thin face. His eyes were bloodshot, dull from weariness. His voice was hoarse. "Bringing him here, Mara, saves the trouble of going after him!"

Calmly Clay said, "He brought me."

The man hardly heard it. Markham's tired, bitter rage broke at Matt Kilgore. "You damned horsethief!"

Clay swung his horse, watching Markham and the men beyond Markham. They had Markham's anger, a dull, exhausted, unreasoning anger, as explosive as powder ready to blow. Kilgore sat his horse straight and unmoved.

"It's a trip I'd rather not have made," said Kilgore without emotion. "You've got right to call me a thief until I speak my side. I rode over to tell it, an' talk reason."

"Reason?" Gid Markham broke in disdainfully, as his hand dropped to his gun holster.

"Easy," Clay said. Markham's bloodshot eyes swung to him. Clay's revolver barrel rested across a leg. "You heard him," he said mildly. "He wants to talk reason, whatever that is."

Kilgore looked around in visible surprise. Markham's stare jumped to Clay's face. "So you chose up sides?"

Clay said, "I never had sides. I helped old Ira Bell for a few days, but my side is all I'm interested in."

"Then get off the ranch!"

"No reason in that," Clay said, "because I'm holding this gun on you. And the first one of those tired, touchy men of yours—or you, either—who pulls a gun, gets blowed off the ranch first." Clay added, "That's reason!"

Markham's hand left his holster and his gaze swung to Matt Kilgore. His bitterness had the rage of a man who had brooded and made his decisions.

"Eighty-two horses, Kilgore, stolen at the Red Rocks. And a trail of dead horses for thirty miles the other side of the Red Rocks. They were changing horses as they rode, killing horses, traveling too fast for us. But on the way back we found one of them that this man Mara had shot at the

110

lava dikes. And his horse. And the horse had your neck brand, Kilgore! Pins all of it straight on you."

Calmly Clay asked, "Get our saddles?"

"Yes! And buried the man!"

Slowly Matt Kilgore said, "Some of that I know. The rest I can guess. Which is why I rode over to talk."

"My father," Gid Markham flung back in bitter animosity, "never talked to horsethieves. I never did. We hung 'em, we shot 'em! A thief is a thief."

"That I've never denied," Kilgore said. "I've felt the same. But there's more to this—"

Kilgore broke off, glancing at the wide side *portal* of the house. And Clay had the queer thought that Gid Markham had passed completely out of Kilgore's mind.

A woman was coming off the *portal,* one hand holding her skirt off hasty, free steps of small feet. She looked younger than Matt Kilgore. She was slender, straight, proud-looking in the black dress which appeared to be fine China silk, and probably was. A narrow white collar formed a small V around the slender column of her neck.

Matt Kilgore's hand swept off his hat. Gid Markham turned impatiently to the woman, but his words were courteous. "Mother, this isn't a woman's business."

She came on to the head of Kilgore's horse, and Matt Kilgore spoke slowly, looking down at her, hat in his hand.

"A long time, Consuela."

She was a native, Clay saw and his years in Central America had given him further insight. Her features were delicate, with born pride, self-possession, and more than a hint even now of the real beauty she must have had in younger years.

Looking up, she said quietly, "A long time, Matthew. Have you come to see me?"

"Not exactly, Connie. There's big trouble to be settled. I rode over to try."

"The horses?"

"That's part of it."

"Mother," said Gid Markham, "I'll—"

Not taking her eyes off Matt Kilgore, she said, "Gideon, be quiet." And he was quiet in dark frustration.

111

Clay pushed his revolver back into the holster, folded hands on the saddle horn and watched with interest. Here ran currents deeper than his knowledge.

Slowly Kilgore said, "A man in my crew named Doyle sneaked off with some men who'd heard Ira Bell was bringing horses south by the Red Rocks. This man Mara was helpin' Ira. They lost the herd to Doyle's bunch. Today Mara spotted Doyle at our place and tangled with him. It was the first thing I knew about it."

No mention of Travis, Clay noted. Kilgore took the blame, shielded the fellow.

Consuela's glance went to Clay's face where raw scratches and bruises still showed. "A very big tangle, I think," she said with faint amusement.

Kilgore spoke earnestly. "Connie, I'll make up the horses. Any way I can, I'll make it right."

"I know you will, Matthew."

Gid Markham broke in with hard bitterness. "More to this than horses! He's got his man Travis now. We had a first warning about Travis, and I knew it, when Travis bailed him out of that bank note. They're hiring men. Making plans! Give 'em an inch and they'll crowd us now."

Matt Kilgore said, "Connie, that ain't all I came for. It's time to live in peace. If there's promises I can make that will hold peace, I'll make 'em to you. If there can't be friendship, we can live quiet, at least. Time for it all to end."

An angry sweep of Gid Markham's hand gestured all of it away. His mother looked at him. "Gideon, what has Matthew Kilgore ever done to you?"

"All my life—"

Her low voice said, "All your life Amos Markham filling you with dislike and hate of Matthew Kilgore."

"He knew—"

"Enough, Gideon," she said quietly. "It is over." She looked up at Matt Kilgore. "You know, Matthew, that when Amos died, the law gave me most of the property. This is my ranch now. This is my house. Will you come in and rest before you start back? And your young friend, of course."

"Ma'am, I thank you," said Clay. His ghost of a smile

112

was for her eyes. "But I've got to get back to Soledad."

The creases in Matt Kilgore's leathery face were deepening in a broad smile. Consuela Markham smiled faintly back at him.

The smallest pulse, Clay noted, beat faster in her neck. She looked younger. Matt Kilgore looked younger, too, with the smile lighting his face under the shock of gray hair as he lightly dismounted. Clay had the feeling that Gid Markham, and all the crew and himself, had passed completely from Kilgore's thoughts. The two of them walked to the *portal* together. Matt Kilgore said something that made her laugh as she looked up at him.

Slowly Clay gathered the reins and eyed the mixed feelings on Gid Markham's face.

"Now that's real reason," Clay said, and swung his horse and left.

18

This was fear such as Patricia Kilgore had never known, nightmarish because of her desperate uncertainty. In the quiet of the big house, through the dragging afternoon hours, the feeling at times approached terror.

Through the kitchen windows she watched the wagons pulling out one by one, each wagon heavily loaded under masking tarps, pulled by four horses, heading obviously into rough country. Riders accompanied each wagon. Some were laughing, talking. Others were silent, as if grim expectancy had dropped upon them.

Each time that Roger walked to the house, Patricia retreated to her bedroom. Late in the afternoon Roger came to her closed bedroom door. His voice was touched with impatience.

"Anything wrong, Pat?"

"A headache."

"Can I open the door?"

"It's bolted," said Patricia steadily. "I'll come to the kitchen."

In the kitchen, she found Roger wearing a plain canvas jacket, jeans, gunbelt, like one of the crew. He was big, hard, confident as his critical look surveyed her.

"You look pale, Pat."

Her smile felt like a stiff grimace. "Where are the wagons going, Roger?"

"I'm starting some fencing." His cool assurance held authority. *As if he owns the ranch now.* "I'll be gone for a day or so," Roger said. "Matt can look for me over by the Ojo Rojo Spring."

"Does Dad know you're starting all this?"

"I decided it was time," Roger said carelessly.

Patricia forced her steady glance on Roger's long bold face and hair shading to the reddish side. "I'm worried about Matt riding over to the Markhams with that man Mara."

"I tried to stop Matt. He would be bullheaded," Roger said without concern. The new authority was strong in Roger. Obviously Matt's movements or wishes did not greatly matter now.

Patricia thought of the warranty deed she had so lightly, recklessly signed. . . . Half the ranch now belonged to Roger. He bulked big and confident in the quiet kitchen, forceful impatience strong on his long-boned face. *Like a stranger now.* Patricia clenched hands when Roger stepped close and kissed her. She held the smile as he walked to the door, spurs chinking, and lifted his hand as he went out.

What has happened to us? Panic, fright increased. *And Matt—what of Matt?*

Sometime after dark Matt returned, whistling in unmistakable cheerfulness as he off-saddled at the corrals. Through the open kitchen door Patricia listened incredulously to that light-hearted, keening whistle. She had hot coffee and warm food on the table when Matt walked in, grinning broadly.

"Everything's going to be all right now," said Matt right off. "Connie Markham an' me settled it all."

114

"What about Gid Markham?"

Matt stopped at the table, caught up the mug of coffee, swallowed deeply, and grinned across the mug. "Connie owns most of that ranch now. What Connie says is what's done."

"Is that man Mara at their ranch?" Patricia inquired with tight care.

"He rode on to Soledad." Matt chuckled as he sat down, his hat pushed back and tilted a little. "Mara wasn't one of Gid's men. He an' his partner helped old Ira Bell out with a hoss herd for a few days, which is how he got pulled into this."

Under her breath, Patricia said, "Two of them! Partners! Where are they from?"

Matt broke open a biscuit and started to butter it. "Drifters, I reckon." His grin came again. "That Mara is all man. I take to him."

Patricia turned to the stove and aimlessly moved the heavy iron skillet. "Roger has taken the wagons out. You can find him around the Ojo Rojo Spring."

"Why'd he do that today?" Matt sounded irritated.

"Roger just decided."

"Wasn't no use of such a rush." Then the good nature which Matt had brought back from the Markham ranch took over. "I'll ride out tomorrow an' take charge," Matt decided.

Patricia's throat tightened as she gazed at Matt's creased and smiling face. Tonight he looked younger, he looked happy. The knot of fear tightened. All Patricia could say was, "It has seemed that way."

Matt had a wry thought.

"I left Mara's pipe in the drawer over there. First one goes to town can leave it at the doctor's house."

"I'll take it," said Patricia.

Matt was squinting past the lamp. "Say! You look kinda peaked and tired."

"I've had a headache."

It satisfied Matt as it had Roger. He left the kitchen whistling again under his breath. Patricia gazed after him,

115

marveling at the magic which Consuela Markham had worked.

Amos Markham was dead. Matt was a lonely man. A fantastic thought parted Patricia's lips. . . . *Consuela Markham was still young-looking, really lovely. Matt was still a catch.* Patricia's wry smile came at the thought of Consuela Markham in the family. Then Patricia sat at the table and the fear came starkly at her again. When she finally went to her bedroom, she knew what she must do tomorrow.

Clay slept in Soledad at the Boston House. In the morning he ate again in Ah Wing's, and thought of the man who had wrapped himself in the life of Roger Travis. A clever fellow, completely ruthless, Clay knew now, who would kill to hold what he had.

Clay was watchful when he left the hotel and walked to Mrs. Strance's house. She opened the door when he knocked. Sleeves were rolled back on her slender arms. Stove heat flushed her smooth cheeks.

"Yes, Mr. Mara?"

Hat in hand, Clay gave her an estimating look. "Ma'am, you visited the Kilgore ranch yesterday."

"Do you object?" Her bright hair, piled higher this morning, not pinned so severely, gave her face a new softness.

"Depends on why you went and what you said, ma'am."

Her eyes measured him. "You mean it depends on what I said about you."

"I mean," Clay said, "exactly that."

"Do you still refuse to answer my questions about San Francisco?"

"Some prying women mean well," Clay said, "some don't. Both kinds make trouble. I need to know what you said about me at the Kilgores' yesterday."

"Is it so important?" When he nodded, she said, "I told Patricia that you'd come to me about your sorrel horse."

"That all?"

"Yes."

"If you're a friend of the Kilgores, let it stay that way," Clay said. "Don't talk about me."

Calmly now, Dorothy Strance said, "Why not?"

116

"Because," said Clay, "you won't know what you're talking about. A gabbling young lady can put her foot in her pretty mouth and be sorry."

Color deepened in her heat-flushed cheeks. Quiet temper entered her measured words.

"Yesterday, Mr. Mara, I suspected you were a dangerous man. Now I'm certain of it." Her glance surveyed the lithe slackness of his tall figure. "Consuela Markham thinks you are Matt Kilgore's friend. I don't think so."

"Yesterday you went to the Markham ranch also and gabbled about me," Clay guessed.

Coolly Dorothy Strance said, "I go where I please. And after this, come to the *Beacon* office, not my home."

Clay's faint smile weighed her as he turned away. "Ought to wear your hair like that more often," he advised. "Looks pretty."

He had no way of knowing that the young widow Strance stood inside her closed door, smiling ruefully to herself before she shook her head in the way of a woman puzzled and exasperated.

Doctor Halvord's buggy was waiting in front of the doctor's house ready for a round of calls. But in his small parlor, Paul Halvord's craggy face smiled about Howie Quist and Ira Bell.

"No reason why they shouldn't move to the hotel now," Halvord said readily. "Quist should be careful for several days."

"How about Ira Bell?"

"Some of these old-timers," said Halvord, "seem to be able to take anything. Bell has had his rest. He's ready to start another trip, although as his doctor I'd suggest more rest."

"Would some easy riding hurt the old man?"

"Do him good, I believe," said Halvord. His sobering glance studied Clay. "Gid Markham and his men stopped in town yesterday on their way back to the ranch. Trouble with the Kilgores seems probable."

"Matt Kilgore rode over to the Markham ranch yesterday afternoon. All settled."

After a moment, Halvord said quietly, "I'm glad."

117

Twenty minutes later Howie Quist, Clay and Ira Bell stopped at Ah Wing's before they went on to the hotel. Howie wanted a steak. They sat at a back table, and Clay told of his visit to the Kilgore ranch and ride to the Markham ranch. Ira Bell asked an odd question.

"You say Matt Kilgore an' Connie Markham was smilin' when they walked in her house together?" And, when Clay nodded, the old man grinned.

"Does it mean anything?" demanded Clay narrowly. "I need to know everything now."

Ira Bell poked his fork at the steak he had ordered. His faded eyes took on a back-reaching look.

"No young feller ever hit the Valley of the Rio Grande like Matt Kilgore did fresh outa the Army." The memories made Ira Bell cackle under his breath. "Matt was like fire loose in tall grass. When he give them black-eyed *señoritas* his big, laughin' howdee-do, they flustered like a buck rooster had hit the pullet roost."

Clay asked, "Was Mrs. Markham there?"

"She was the proudest, purtiest gal in all the Upper an' Lower River settlements," said Ira Bell. "Only then she was Consuela Rivera. New Mexico never seen the like of them two together." Ira Bell sank his knife into the thick steak and grinned again at his memories.

"Don't hold back on us," said Howie in exasperation. "You got 'em together now."

Again Ira cackled under his breath.

"They was together with winder bars an' distance atween 'em. Lookin' at each other 'crost the street they was together. If Matt hadn't made a trip to Santa Fe, Connie Rivera'd been Miss Pat Kilgore's mamma—an' a fine mamma, too."

Clay remembered the gray-haired man yesterday, watching the slender woman in black walk toward him. "Kilgore went to Santa Fe and met another girl?"

"A man can't he'p what hits him. Matt fetched a wife back from Santa Fe."

Clay's soft whistle came. "Rough on the girl waiting for him."

"Connie understood. Right off, quick, she married Matt's

118

best friend. Matt an' his new wife was at Connie's weddin'—an' the laughin'est one there was Connie."

"What started the feud between Amos Markham and Matt?"

"Ain't outsider's business."

"I mean no harm, old man. But it may help me."

"I ain't fergot I owe you," Bell said. He brooded. "Amos was a Bible man, give to right earnest prayin'. Made him unforgivin' to them as didn't see his way. Ain't it plain Amos knowed he got second choice from Connie, an' it worked on him 'til he give Connie thirty year of sad misery?"

Howie forked a bite of steak and snorted. "Pickin' jealous on his wife thirty year!"

Ira Bell shrugged, and Clay sensed they had not heard all the story. "Do people know this?" Clay asked.

"Most is dead that mighta guessed it. Connie never let on about her misery. She'd made her trade an' stayed proud. Folks never saw much of her."

"I see," said Clay slowly, and he saw many things.

Thirty years with Amos Markham, never complaining, Clay thought. *But she never forgot Matt Kilgore.* Yesterday they were together again.

Then his own hard, uncompromising business moved in. Casually Clay said to Ira Bell, "Like to ride out with me a few days? You know the country."

"I owe you," said Bell readily.

Later, while Bell went on to the hotel, Clay and Howie walked slowly around the plaza. Howie's broad face, shaved now, was showing a trace of healthy color as his tremendous vitality asserted itself.

"Travis has dug in here," said Clay thoughtfully. "He owns half the Kilgore ranch already; he's going to marry Patricia Kilgore. And he's like a son now to Matt Kilgore."

"Hell of a son," muttered Howie.

"Protects him," Clay said. "The Kilgores and all their friends will believe him and back him. We know he's a liar and a thief. And I think he's moved like a thief and liar with honest people, so that he's on loose ground."

"How come?" Howie said alertly.

119

"He had a Socorro lawyer at the ranch," Clay mused. "He let that horsethief Doyle go free. Piles of fence posts are cut and ready, and this isn't fence country. Empty wagons are waiting. A large, tough crew is ready for some sort of trouble."

Frowning, Howie asked, "What kinda trouble?"

"I don't know," Clay admitted. "But I can't see big trouble breaking without Gid Markham being pulled into it. And trouble with Gid Markham is something Matt Kilgore doesn't want now."

"Where does this get us?" said Howie, skeptically.

"Travis is top man with the Kilgores and hard to get at now, short of shooting him," said Clay with slow thought. "But a liar and a thief can hang himself among honest people. If Matt Kilgore ever turns against him, he'd better watch out. I'm going to scout around and see what's about to happen."

"You sure Travis don't suspicion you?"

"Reasonably certain. But the young widow at the newspaper suspects something. She's dangerous."

"Ain't all women?" Howie was increasingly disturbed. "I oughta go with you."

"Not until the doctor says so," Clay flatly refused.

"Then old Bell can name a spot where I c'n find you two in a few days," insisted Howie stubbornly. "I ain't meaning to shank-sit here in town while Travis picks you off."

Clay grinned. "He won't; but come along when you can. Travis is cornered now. Only thing is how best to get him."

19

Patricia's fear this same morning was greater because she dared not share her improbable belief. She watched her father leave for the Ojo Rojo Spring, and Matt's hat had the jaunty tilt of last night. He was whistling lightheartedly.

For a moment Patricia felt gratitude for the new zest for living which Matt obviously had gotten from Consuela Markham. Then, as she slowly re-entered the house, the fear came at her again until it was close to panic. It drove her into Roger's deserted bedroom with tight-lipped purpose.

On the wall, Dick's photograph, young and smiling and forever gone, watched her hurried search of the room.

Among other things, Patricia found a journal wrapped in oiled silk. She carried the packet to her room and, tensely on the edge of her bed, read the closely written pages.

It was a devastating experience.

Written in the journal were all the events which Roger had ever spoken of—but Roger's words had been stilted and unreal, Patricia realized now.

From the pages she turned slowly, came alive a man who never could have been Roger. This man was a surging, vital stranger, lighthearted, humorous. His great hopes and his soaring happiness stirred deep emotions.

And the final agony of his grief and lonely despair far north in Wyoming wrenched at Patricia. Her eyes were damp when she carried the journal back to Roger's room and, for an aching, lonely moment, gazed at Dick's smiling face on the wall. And then, quickly in the mid-morning, Patricia started a hasty, determined ride to Soledad.

When she reached the busy Soledad plaza, she sighted the man named Howie Quist lolling on a bench in the yard of the Boston House. Quist saw her reining up at the hotel tie-rail and came forward. They met at the edge of the sparse yard grass.

Patricia remembered how this big man had sprawled in a gray-faced daze on the sorrel horse. Today, washed and barbered, Quist's broad face had a milder look. His interest was wary as Patricia bluntly inquired, "Is Mr. Mara in the hotel?"

"No, ma'am," he said briefly.

"Where can I find him?"

Estimating her shrewdly, Quist pondered the question. "Clay," he said finally, "rode outa town." And when Patricia impatiently demanded, "Where?" Quist thought that over also. "I ain't exactly sure, ma'am."

121

"When will he be back?"

"Clay didn't rightly know hisself." Quist's stare searched her face. "Somethin' wrong?"

"I don't know." Her question wrenched at him. "Were you ever a coachman?"

Quist said, "Now ain't that a funny question."

"A coachman in San Francisco?"

"Some folks," said Quist vaguely, "get queer ideers. Way off there now, in San Francisco."

Tightly Patricia demanded, "Were you there when a man escaped from a bank by bluffing with a pipe in his pocket? Like this pipe of Clay Mara's?"

Quist's stare narrowed on the pipe which Patricia took from her jacket pocket. His muscular hand reached quickly for the pipe. His manner hardened.

"You've said plenty, young lady. Now say the rest. How'd you know all this?"

Now all her doubts vanished. The surge of Patricia's fear turned into anger as her greenish blue eyes rested on the big, startled Howie Quist.

"Mrs. Strance," said Patricia coldly, "gave a clipping from an old San Francisco newspaper to Roger Travis. It told how the two men escaped after one of them tried to cash a draft against an account in the name of R. Travis."

Quist's harsh question whipped back. "Has Travis seen this pipe?"

"Not yet."

"What's Travis think about Clay Mara an' me?"

"He thinks you both work for Gid Markham. What *are* you two men doing here?"

A slight sheen of perspiration was coming on Quist's forehead. "We was driftin', headin' for Santa Fe when we met old man Bell an' helped him with his hoss herd."

"A likely story." Patricia's straw sombrero barely topped his wide shoulder. The braided *barbiquejo* straps brushed her flushed cheeks as she angrily warned, "Stop covering for this man Mara. I can find him. You might as well tell me!"

"Now, ma'am—"

"Don't 'ma'am' me! Where is he?"

"Take days to find him, maybe." Quist was visibly perspiring. "Let be 'til I c'n find Clay. Take my word for it, ma'am."

"I wouldn't," said Patricia, "take your word that the sun shines. And I've no intention of waiting. I'll find the man!"

Quist stared at her apprehensively. "How'll you find him?" he asked.

"I'm going to Dorothy Strance with all this miserable business," said Patricia recklessly. "Both of us know this country and everyone in it. Mara can't stay out of sight long!"

"Women!" It was close to a groan. "Ain't no use bein' a wildcat. You aim to drag Travis into it?"

"Whatever I decide!" said Patricia hotly, and she walked quickly away to find Dot Strance, leaving Quist mute, sweating and glowering in indecision after her.

In mushy blue twilight, Ira Bell rode down a winding cattle trail over black lava outcroppings. The old man had a gnomelike look as he hunched on the rough-coated, wiry mustang bought cheaply in Soledad. Clay lifted his voice. "No water for fifteen miles. We camping dry tonight?"

Over his shoulder, Bell said in unconcern, "They's water for them as know where to look. Them as don't know, stays dry. Country's like that."

They rode finally into a long swale with a spring-fed waterhole at the upper end. With a blanket apiece, food in their saddlebags, a frying pan, small coffee pot, tin cups, they camped well.

Deer watered in the swale. Coyotes clamored in distance as Clay lay staring up at the spattered stars, thinking of Travis. Anticipation of the end was in him now. . . . And, during the forenoon of the next day, it filled him when they arrived, finally, at the small *placita* of Piedras.

Immense old cottonwoods ringed the settlement. A lumbering cart with wheels of tree trunk rounds rimmed with iron bands creaked past behind six diminutive mouse-colored burros. Dogs barked. Women with faces covered to bright, curious eyes with the black shawls called *rebozos* watched them ride between the low adobe huts into a small bare plaza.

123

Men called greetings in Spanish to Ira Bell.

"Knowed some of them since they was shirt-bare kids abeggin' for them little brown-sugar cones called *piloncillo* I usta buy 'em," said Ira Bell, grinning. "They're close-mouthed with strangers, but they'll talk t' me."

A small adobe store of sorts across the plaza had a short, sagging hitchrack and a narrow *portal* holding up-ended boxes. Men were walking toward them as they dismounted before the store.

Ira Bell called in Spanish, "Gregorio! *Como le va?* Juanito! *Com' 'sta?"* and to Clay, "Somethin' up here!"

"Look!" said Clay. Howie Quist was emerging from the store.

"Knowed he wouldn't lay around Soledad," Ira Bell said, and walked to meet his Piedras friends.

Piedras was where Howie was to have joined them later on. Howie came off the store *portal* with relief on his broad face and concern in his question. "You had any trouble yet?"

Clay's welcoming grin was wry. "Trouble now, with you on our hands. Told you to get strong before you left town."

"That redheaded widow an' the Kilgore gal," Howie blurted, "is fixin' to throw you to Travis!" And, as Clay's face tightened, Howie gave Clay the pipe and grimly recounted his talk with Patricia Kilgore. "I been waitin' here since yesterday, not knowin' where to find you two, or if Travis'd get you first!"

"That widow!" said Clay softly. His rueful, remembering smile came. "She evidently knew about the South Bay Bank the other morning when I lighted my pipe in her yard. No wonder she jabbed at me about San Francisco. Howie, never trust a redheaded woman."

"Any woman," said Howie dismally. "A taffy-haired gal done me dirt."

Intently Clay asked, "Patricia Kilgore said Travis had seen the clipping—but hadn't seen my pipe?"

"She was breathin' blue fire an' threats," said Howie glumly. "She lit out for the widder, meanin' to find you, get hold of Travis, too, an' no tellin' what."

Ira Bell had been shaking hands and talking with the dark-

124

featured men of the *placita*. Gestures and blurts of liquid Spanish were rapid as the men walked out of the plaza with Ira.

Howie said, "This place has been buzzin' all mornin'. Yesterday they was friendly. Today they been treatin' me like a robber bee who snuck in the hive. I been wonderin' if Travis or the Kilgores is back of it."

"Ira will find out," Clay said. He rolled a smoke slowly and stood in frowning intentness. And, a little later, when Ira Bell returned alone, they both waited expectantly.

"Let's get goin'," said Ira, briefly. He held silence until Howie got his horse from behind the store and they were riding out of the small plaza. "I talked to a feller who had a bullet in his leg," Ira said then. "Tried to water his hoss at sun-up over on Mesa Blanca. Homesteaders without wimmen or kids was fencin' land around the water. They shot his leg afore he got away."

Alertly, Clay said, "Homesteaders without women?"

"Uh-huh. They's been surveyin' in these parts, too, quiet-like. Piedras folks paid no mind, figurin' 'twas Markham business."

"Is this Mesa Blanca on Markham land?"

"Yep. Men rode quick to tell Gid."

Frowning, Clay said, "What made homesteaders think they could dig in on Markham land?"

Ira Bell shrugged as he swung his rough-coated mustang into a dirt lane skirting small irrigated fields. "It ain't legal-like Gid's land. It's open land."

"I thought Mrs. Markham inherited Spanish Grant land, and Amos Markham added to it," Clay said quickly.

"Connie's land wasn't great shucks," said Ira carelessly. "Amos spread over free range that nobody wanted them days. Matt Kilgore done the same, although Matt bought up water rights when he could."

Ruefully, Clay said, "Start thinking from the wrong facts, and you come out all wrong. I thought all this was owned land."

"The feller who can hold it uses it," Ira said. "There ain't water, hardly, for cattle, let alone crops. Connie Markham

125

understood these Piedras folks. They was satisfied for Amos to spread all around. But strangers now, fencin' off, shootin'—"

Clay mused with growing conviction, "Ten, fifteen miles and more between water. Own the land legally around the water, and the free land everywhere else is useless to others." And, when Ira nodded agreement, Clay said narrowly, "You're sure the Markhams claim this Mesa Blanca water?"

"They've used it twenty-five year an' more."

"How far from here?"

"Coupla hours."

Clay made a quick decision. "I need to see who's fencing that water. Lead off."

"You got shot at fer me. My turn, I reckon." Bell looked resigned as he swung the mustang off the dirt lane away from the last of the small, irrigated fields.

Less than two hours later the sun was almost straight up when they dropped off pine-dotted uplands into a tangle of ridges and draws where chokeberry bushes grew. They climbed out of a draw, threaded brush and lichen-spotted rocks and glimpsed open country ahead. In a rock-rimmed pocket spilling down at the far end, Bell pulled up. His wrinkled face was calm.

"We'll be clost, quick now, sneakin' on 'em from cover."

Clay jacked a shell into his carbine. "I'll have my look alone." He walked the cat-footed black gelding on out of the pocket, twisting down through rocks and brush into a grassy bay from which he looked over a wide, rolling mesa.

Howie and Ira Bell had followed him. Clay motioned them back, dismounted and advanced on foot. At his right a rocky finger ridge reached out a hundred yards. When he cleared the ridge, the spring-fed waterhole was on to the right not two hundred yards distant. A wagon was there. Four men were setting fence posts. And the man who looked up and sighted Clay's solitary figure yelled warning. All four men dived for rifles they had close on the ground.

The first man who faced Clay bawled, "A water right is filed here, legal an' regular! No business of any Markham man! Get goin'!"

126

The man at the left, swinging fast, bringing up his carbine, bawled, "Use them raafles!"

It was the burly Doyle, and Clay's great grin of satisfaction—and relief, too—had nothing to do with the gunfire suddenly on him. He dropped flat as Doyle shot. The thin wail of the bullet close overhead was blotted by the breaching report of Clay's carbine firing back. And by the gunshots of Doyle's companions, and guns opening up behind Clay.

When the swift flurry of shots died away, Doyle and the other three men had gone to earth also. And, behind Clay, Howie's exasperated protest lifted. "You ride two hours here to get your head shot off?"

"Had enough, Howie? Keep 'em down!" Clay called over a shoulder.

Howie fired. The guns at the waterhole drove angry shots back. And Clay scrambled up, dodging, running for the shelter of the finger ridge. Howie and Ira Bell hugged rocks and pumped shots at the waterhole to cover his run. Clay pulled up grinning, panting in the sheltered pocket where he had started.

Sourly Howie called, "Ain't it fun?"

"Get out of here!" Clay ordered. Their horses were there, and when the three of them were riding back up through the rock-rimmed pocket, Clay called to Ira Bell, "How far to the Kilgore house?"

"Couple more hours."

"Make it fast," Clay directed. And to Howie, Clay called jubilantly, "Like I thought, Travis has cut his own ground out from under him! I've got him now, Howie!"

20

The high, hard humor was still in Clay when they pulled the sweating horses to a brief walk across a sun-drenched, high country meadow. Howie, riding at Clay's left, speculated, "I wonder if any other Markham waterholes is bein' fenced?"

At Clay's right, Ira Bell said calmly, "Gid'll run 'em all out fast."

"He'll try," Clay said, "and he'll get the surprise of his life. You heard the man yell that a water right had been filed. Those men were at the Kilgore ranch when I was there, which is what I wanted to make sure. Travis is moving in on Gid Markham with the law behind him and a big gun crew to back the law."

Bell's sunken eyes looked over uncertainly. "Heerd you say in Soledad that Matt Kilgore promised Connie Markham no more trouble, ever."

"Travis didn't say so. He's half-owner of Kilgore's ranch now."

Hunched on the rough-coated mustang, Bell pushed black kerchief folds up over his face in a tired gesture. The old man's words had a kind of unbelieving wonder.

"If Gid's waterholes is fenced off, then Gid'll have to pull everything he owns outa the country quick. Thirty years here—an' finished in days!"

Levelly Clay said, "It's started now."

"Then sure as cats jump blue rats, Gid'll kill Matt Kilgore like Amos planned all along," said Ira Bell in slow dismay.

Clay said sharply, "In Soledad the other day, old man, you held back about Amos Markham and Matt Kilgore, didn't you? Now what's the real truth?"

Intently Clay watched a clouding, back-reaching look enter Bell's tired eyes. "The night Gid was born," Bell said simply, "I was waitin' in the house with Amos. We both heerd Connie cry out Matt's name."

Clay's soft whistle did not stop Bell's reluctant words. "Hell jumped black in Amos. Fierce he asked me how clost Matt an' Connie really was afore Matt got married sudden, and Connie married Amos hasty right after."

Carefully, Clay said, "Well—how close?"

"Amos wronged a proud little lady who only cried out lonely an' helpless fer the man she really loved," said Bell's tired voice. "An' it nailed her to a cross she never got loose from. Amos was wild that night. He got out his Bible an'

128

told me his own name of Amos meant a feller who had a burden to bear. An' Matthew meant a gift from the Lord. It made proof to Amos right there his suspicions was Bible fact."

"And Amos planned?" prodded Clay intently.

Slowly Bell said, "That night Amos, black an' bitter, named the baby boy Gideon. Said it meant a killer. An' I watched him raise Gid to hate Matt Kilgore enough to kill Matt some day."

"The man," Clay said in short distaste, "was black crazy. Does Matt Kilgore know this?"

"Nope . . . Connie does. Thirty year she lived with it, proud an' silent." Bell stared at the ground. "Today Amos'll be happy."

Clay halted his walking horse. His slow smile considered Howie and Ira Bell, who reined up also.

"Today we'll make Amos Markham real unhappy while he roasts," Clay promised. "Matt Kilgore isn't fencing Markham waterholes. Doyle wouldn't ever be working for Kilgore. Travis is doing this—and it's cutting Travis loose from Kilgore. Makes Travis my man now!"

Howie dubiously said, "Could be wrong."

"My guess, my risk," said Clay, still smiling. He felt that way now, anticipating and confident as he weighed Howie and Bell. This last hard riding had sapped both men. "Both of you are too tuckered for more hard riding. Old man, point me the straight way to the Kilgore house. You two come on easy." He cut off Howie's protest. "Might need you later, Howie. Don't give out on me now." Grumbling, Howie reluctantly subsided.

And, nearly an hour later, when Clay rode his sweating, blowing horse into the big yard behind the Kilgore house, he saw that all the wagons were gone. The armed crew had departed. Two horses were in the nearest corral, and Clay cleared his gun holster as he rode to the back of the house.

He was dismounting when the Widow Strance appeared in the kitchen doorway. Clay's hand left his holster, and his tightening humor took in her plain riding skirt and jacket.

"Still prying around, ma'am?" Her smooth cheeks flushed. Clay grinned. "Matt Kilgore here?"

"No."

"Travis then?"

"Nor Travis," said Dorothy Strance so coldly that Clay laughed and brought out the pipe which Howie had given him.

"I'll help you print it now, ma'am. I'm the one who walked out of the South Bay Bank."

Her reply was biting. "I know what to print. It will be headed: *The Thief From San Francisco!*"

"That," Clay said, "should pop your lady readers' eyes."

"I knew you meant trouble," said Dorothy Strance with open dislike. "But I didn't suspect you must have come to help Roger Travis and Matt Kilgore in the boldest steal Socorro County has ever known!"

Clay's stare went quizzical before his wry grin slowly came. "I told you in Soledad, ma'am, that a prying young lady would get her foot in her pretty mouth." Her color deepened and Clay drawled, "I'll let it stay in your mouth. Where's Miss Kilgore?"

"Patricia is riding to find her father. He should have been back by now. He has a visitor. Mrs. Markham is here."

Clay stopped smiling.

"I'll wait for Kilgore," he said quietly. He led the froth-flecked black gelding toward the log watering trough and heard the kitchen door close with force behind him.

While the gelding drank, Clay checked his revolver and carbine for what was surely coming. And coming swiftly now. He carefully reset the saddle. After rolling a smoke, he strolled restlessly about the deserted yard. . . . Some time later when he sighted the solitary rider coming leisurely, he guessed that Patricia had missed her father. Matt Kilgore obviously was unaware of the visitors in the house.

Clay strolled to the kitchen door. Kilgore's creased, keen smile estimated him as the man rode up. "Come for that pipe, Mara?" Before Clay could answer, the door opened. Kilgore blurted, "Connie!" and swung quickly off the horse.

For the moment Clay forgot all else. Consuela Markham ignored him as she came out into the warm sunlight. Slender in her black serge riding habit, the small-boned, proud oval of her face was pale as she spoke to Matt Kilgore.

130

"Thirty years, Matthew—" She had to stop, swallow before her low voice went on, "Always, like a candle in a dark night that had no end, there was Matthew Kilgore to believe in." Her hand made a relinquishing gesture. "Now that is gone. What can I ever believe in again?"

Hat in his square, rope-burned hand, Kilgore stared blankly from the saddle at her. Bewilderment cut deeper lines in his weathered face. "What's happened, Connie?"

"I believed your promise of no more trouble. Now you're fencing waterholes!"

"We're spreadin' out, Connie, beyond the Ojo Rojo Spring."

"You're fencing water we've always used. You're taking my ranch and driving me out!"

"No, Connie. Orders has got mixed."

She was proud, she was slender and scornful as she looked up at the bewildered man.

"Don't lie to me again, Matthew! Before I started here a friend had just arrived from Socorro, killing horses to reach us. All this country, he said, has been quietly surveyed. Strange men have filed applications in the Land Office at Las Cruces for homestead titles and water rights. The court at Socorro has been asked for an injunction to stop us from interfering, and a hearing has been set. And every lawyer in Socorro has been hired by you, Matthew, so we can't even have a lawyer to help us!"

And, as Kilgore stared blankly, her low voice went on: "Now Gideon will kill you—or you will kill Gideon!" Sadness, bewilderment, pain broke from her. "Why, Matthew? Why this to me?"

Matt spoke quietly, his voice low but determined. "I don't say trust me now, Connie, because I guess you won't. Just wait here while I ride out an' look into this."

"While you go to this man Travis who has become another son?" She stood straighter, taller. "I waited thirty years. Now Gideon is my hope. Take warning, Matthew—nothing will hold Gideon back now!"

Kilgore's hand made a helpless gesture as he turned away from her.

Clay spoke then. "I'll ride with you."

131

From the saddle, Kilgore's reply was coldly stern. "I got enough to handle. You follow me, stranger, and I'll gun you down! This is my business!"

And the man would, Clay saw, and hesitated. He had no quarrel with this stern, stricken man who was being ground and torn between loyalties and emotions. Calmly, Clay warned, "Watch Travis. He's dangerous now."

The stare Matt Kilgore gave him was stern and expressionless as the man wheeled his horse and rode away.

The fear was a great wave in Patricia as she rode to find her father, and the pale face of Consuela Markham haunted her.

Ahead on the shimmering grass flats, prairie dogs stood upright on their dirt mounds in poker-stiff alarm, and flashed down out of sight as the hard run of Patricia's roan horse came at them, and swerved to miss the treacherous holes. The fear in Patricia grew to near-terror again as she thought of this unbelievable thing which was happening to Matt and herself.

Using twisting, grassy draws when possible, Patricia crossed a belt of timbered hills. A time or two she drove the roan directly up through heavy oak brush, ignoring the slapping, clawing branches. Her mind stayed on the pale woman waiting back at the house, and the wild retaliation which Gid Markham was planning even now.

The rider Patricia finally sighted swung his horse to meet her, and he was not Matt. He was one of the crew, a lank, rough-looking man with a black mustache whose name Patricia did not even know.

"Your old man's ridin' to the house," he told her. "Travis is at Cow Springs."

"Cow Springs is on Markham land!" Patricia threw at him.

His grin was thin. "Wouldn't know, ma'am." But he did know, of course.

Patricia left him gazing after her, and pointed the roan toward Cow Springs, driven now by resentful anger. Matt would find Consuela Markham at the house and would quickly know what was happening. And Matt—*how well she knew Matt*—would ride to find Roger Travis. And Matt would still be ignorant of what he should know.

Desperately now Patricia wished that she had told Matt everything. And told Dorothy Strance. This, now, was the best she could think to do.

The yucca was in bloom on Cow Springs Mesa. Tall flower stalks lifted masses of white, bell-shaped blooms tinged with purple, which the natives called Our Lord's Candles. Patricia had never tired of the sight each spring and early summer. Today she ignored the flowers on every side and rode toward the ridges east of the mesa and the grassy pocket where the springs started a shallow, meandering little stream which died away in its own scant sands halfway across the mesa.

Two wagons, fence posts, staked horses, waiting men were at the springs. The man who stepped on a horse and rode to meet her was Roger Travis, looking big and formidable in canvas jacket, jeans, gunbelt and black hat. Roger's long, rugged face when they met had the smiling force and assurance so much a part of him.

"Lonesome back at the house?" Roger greeted her lightly.

Patricia said, "No." Her eyes dwelt in fascination on the sunlight brightening strong auburn tints in Roger's hair. "You're fencing Markham water, Roger!"

"That's right," said Roger calmly.

"Matt won't have it!"

"Why, I think he will." *Cool, confident, the new authority.* "This is for Matt too, and us, Pat. Part of my plans."

Patricia loosened the braided leather *barbiquejo* straps under her chin. She tried desperately to appear calm. "Not for Matt! Not for me! What are you trying to do, Roger? Who are you?"

Roger's smile did not change. "Remember me, Pat? The man you're going to marry?"

Her mouth was dry. "The man I thought I was going to marry went to Central America through San Francisco. But you've never been there, Roger, have you?"

Roger said nothing until he lighted a cigar and bent the match carelessly between fingers, watching her. Then he was so amused and easy that Patricia almost could have believed

133

him. "I had my reasons for saying so. Is that all that's worrying you, darling?"

"No," Patricia said. "That isn't worrying me. What is, Roger, is who you really are."

He held the amusement, eyebrows lifting. "I don't understand."

"Neither do I," said Patricia evenly. "Because, you see, Roger, you have reddish hair and blue eyes. And Dick's partner in Central America had dark-brown hair and gray eyes. Dick's last letter to me telling about his new partner said so. I'd forgotten it until I read the letter again." Suddenly it broke inside her, tearing at her control, so that the words wrenched at him. *"Who are you? Did you kill my brother? What are you doing here with us?"*

Little points of cold determination flashed in Roger's eyes. His solid force hardened into icy calm.

"You're hysterical, Pat. Who notices hair and eyes accurately? Hair changes color." And, fiercely, he said, "How much money do I have to spend on you and Matt to prove who I am?"

It rushed from her, choking, reckless.

"Tell it to the man who tried to draw money from the Travis account in San Francisco! He has dark-brown hair and gray eyes! And the pipe he used to escape from the bank!"

Too late now. It was said. Appalled, Patricia watched muscles bunching in Roger's cheeks. Past Roger in the distance where the crew waited she recognized the burly man named Grady Doyle whom Clay Mara had beaten and Roger claimed to have fired. *Roger had lied also about firing Doyle.*

And Roger, with a cold blaze in his eyes, was swinging his horse in close, catching the reins of her horse. Roger's voice was thin. "Dark-brown hair and gray eyes? Did that fellow Clay Mara have a straight-stemmed pipe?"

For breathless seconds Patricia gazed at Roger's fiercely demanding face—and her conviction came suddenly, *he's afraid,* leaving her startled that Roger could be afraid of anything. Then when Patricia remembered the bronzed, hard stranger named Clay Mara, she could understand Roger's fear. And suddenly she clung to that memory of Clay Mara

134

as a surprising shield and source of strength. *After disliking him, fearing him.*

"He had the pipe," Patricia said. Thinking only of Matt's safety now, she said, "Talk to Mara if you can find him. And let go of my reins! The men are watching."

Roger drew a slow breath. "I can find him," he said thinly. "Mara was at Mesa Blanca a short while ago. A man just got here and told me." Roger's smile came with obvious effort, smoothing out the bunched muscles along his jaw as he released the reins. "You've made a great mistake, Pat. We'll straighten it out."

"I hope so," Patricia said with forced calm. "Now will you stop fencing Markham water?"

"I'll talk to Matt."

"Then I'll get back to the house." *Would Roger stop her as the roan gelding swung away?*

An easy trot, a slow lope . . . Could Roger guess the frantic urge to reach Matt, and stop Matt from any clash of temper with this dangerous man who called himself Roger Travis? This man who had held her close and kissed her and spoken of his need for her.

Patricia did not look back. . . . *Clay Mara had just been to Mesa Blanca. Why?* Had he been hunting Roger? Would Roger hunt him now?

The masses of creamy yucca blooms fell behind as Patricia rode off the mesa. Her last look back showed Roger walking his horse to his men, head bowed in deep thought. And suddenly Patricia knew what Roger was planning, what he would do as cold-bloodedly as he must have planned everything else. When the first rise hid her, she swung the leather quirt and drove the roan into a reckless, frantic run.

21

Travis had always despised weakness. His face was aggressively hard when he reined up at the two wagons and called, "Doyle! Where did that Mara and the two men with him go?"

"West from Mesa Blanca; toward Soledad looked like."

The twelve men lounging around the wagons and steaming coffee pot on the smoking cook fire embers were heavily armed and tough. This was the fighting bunch Travis was holding here at Cow Springs to meet any retaliation Markham tried. They had seen Patricia, they were visibly curious as Travis rubbed his right palm on the rough jean cloth of his leg, drying the sweat of tension.

"This Mara," said Travis, levelly, "made trouble at the ranch, too. He's a Markham gunman. He'll kill too many of you if he's not stopped."

A man at the cook fire reminded, "You had him cold-turkey at the ranch and let 'im go!"

"Matt Kilgore took him back to Markham!" The memory of Matt's bullheaded folly sharpened the order Travis gave. "Every man will stop work wherever he is and hunt this man Mara. You men ride to the other camps and tell them. I'll take charge of it from the Kilgore house." As they stirred, some starting to grin, Travis added, "A thousand dollars cash for Mara dead! Two thousand if he's dead by noon tomorrow!"

That was the bait which would make every man dangerous. Soft whistles, blurted oaths, instant attention proved it. Grady Doyle's blue-black left eye still had a trace of squint as Doyle called, "How about them two with Mara?"

Travis remembered the San Francisco newspaper clipping, and the coachman who had helped the man escape from the

136

South Bay Bank. He guessed now that the coachman must be the one named Howie Quist who had come with Mara. Old Ira Bell, too, might know the story.

"Same for them," said Travis shortly. "I'll add five hundred extra for Mara. Now get going. You, Doyle, ride with me."

Minutes later when Travis rode away with Doyle, the camp was breaking up, men saddling swiftly, talking, laughing, making plans. By sundown all the armed crew would be combing the country clear to Soledad.

And now the sweating shock of Patricia's words moved in. The tremendous mockery of what had happened to him descended on Travis as he thought of the bronzed stranger who had faced him in the Kilgore kitchen. *The real Roger Travis.* And he had struck the man down himself, and had tried to hire him. And had watched Mara walk away safely with Matt Kilgore. When Travis recalled how the man had almost destroyed Grady Doyle with bare hands, the sweating tension became almost unbearable.

Grady Doyle rode close now, protesting, "I ain't layin' around the ranchhouse, with all that money offered for a little raafle shootin'!"

Travis coldly reminded, "Mara got away from you twice, and beat you senseless at the ranch. You'll probably run at sight of him. I want you to ride to that line cabin and see if any of your gunmen are back to help."

"For that money," said Doyle, going sullen, "they'd hunt down Gid Markham."

"Markham's turn," Travis promised, "will come later."

The churning thoughts caught him again. Matt Kilgore, he had no doubt, could be handled easily enough. The bond between Matt and himself was too strong to be broken now. And, when this man Mara was trapped, Patricia's doubts could be talked away. But the thoughts now of what he stood to lose were overwhelming.

In anger and resentment, Travis remembered the day he had stood in the Bonanza Bar laughing and content, friends around him, and Patricia eagerly waiting outside. That had been the last carefree hour. Since then nothing had gone quite right. . . . Now this frantic need to kill a man blotted out everything else. Travis wondered where this Clay Mara was now.

At the weathered adobe back of the Kilgore house, Clay Mara watched the slender woman in black stand motionless while her gaze followed the spurred run of Matt Kilgore's horse into the shimmering distance. She seemed to droop a little as she turned slowly back to the kitchen doorway where Dorothy Strance watched her with a pitying look.

Clay spoke to her. "Ma'am, Kilgore told you the truth. He didn't know about this. Travis is fencing your water."

Consuela Markham paused, seemingly aware of him for the first time. Color touched her pallor. "You know this?"

"Why should I tell you wrong?"

"Dorothy believes you are helping them."

"Dorothy," said Clay, "has got her mind on too many things." When red showed in Dot Strance's smooth cheeks, Clay grinned at her and spoke to Gid Markham's mother. "Travis is a liar and a thief but he owns half this ranch now. I heard you ask Matt Kilgore what you could ever believe in again."

She said, "Yes," watching him intently.

"Why not try believing in Kilgore again?" Clay suggested. "He's got Travis to deal with. Your son Gid will be hunting him. Kilgore needs some faith today."

She said slowly, "You believe in Matthew, don't you, young man?"

Clay's small smile came. "Haven't known him long—not thirty years. But he'll do for me."

It was something to see—her irresolution and doubt, her hunger to believe becoming conviction, putting life and sparkle into her eyes.

Under her breath, Consuela Markham vowed, "And he will for me!" Her own small smile gave him gratitude; then worry knit her fine arched brows. "Why did you not tell Matthew all this about Travis?"

"A man like Kilgore," said Clay, "has to find out for himself before he believes."

"Gideon," she said under her breath, "took his armed

138

men toward Piedras! From there he will hunt Matthew. I know Gideon. He must be told this!" Her eyes begged. "Can you—?"

"No, ma'am," Clay refused. He adjusted his gunbelt before walking to his horse. "Travis is the man I want. Kilgore will find him. And I'll follow Kilgore to him."

He had underestimated this slender woman whose eyes were bright now with something which was singing inside.

"Then," she said, "I will follow you to Matthew and stay with him until he is safe." And quietly she said something that only Clay understood. "It will not happen as Amos planned!"

Thinking of that night thirty years ago, and all that had happened to her since, Clay said, "I'll saddle your horse." To Dorothy Strance in the doorway he said, "Gid Markham may come here with his crew. If anyone can hold him here waiting, maybe you can." Malice touched his advice. "If you hold Gid tight enough and long enough."

He had his reward in the flush which again suffused her face as he turned away. . . . And the ranchhouse was behind them when Consuela Markham, riding lightly and easily with him, called over, "Is this man Travis really dangerous?"

"He is," said Clay, watching the shod horse tracks he was following.

"And you want him?"

"I've come a long way to find him."

"Why?"

"You wouldn't believe it, ma'am."

"So many things I once would not believe," she said. "So much I want to believe now."

And, because the end was close now and nothing could hold it back, and Matt Kilgore would have need of all her understanding, Clay told her. . . . Soberly, as they rode, he gave her the truth about the man who called himself Roger Travis.

At the end, she said, "A strange story—but I believe it because I think Patricia knows it already." To Clay's swift look, she said, "Patricia was already afraid today when Dorothy and I reached the house. It was in her eyes." Consuela Markham hesitated. "A girl in love and happy," she said, "would not cry, 'How could he have done this to us?'"

"I've asked myself the same thing," Clay said. "He had my money, my name, even my memories—everything."

With conviction, she said, "You will have your name back."

They were in rolling country with ridges ahead. The long-spaced tracks of Kilgore's running horse had dug in deep through here, easily followed. Clay's gaze swept the distance before he replied.

"More back than my name. I've been adding up all I've learned. His bank account is in my name, under my signature which he copied. His certificates of deposit from St. Louis are in my name. He put his half of the Kilgore ranch in my name." Clay smiled thinly across at her. "It'll take time, but I can prove who I am. All the rest is waiting here. Travis didn't mean to—but he started my life over for me. We're neighbors, ma'am. You won't even have to use a new name. I'm Roger Travis."

The look Consuela Markham gave him held the secret smiling thoughts of an older woman.

"Has it occurred to you," she asked, "that other things have been started for you which no true *caballero* could refuse to honor?"

Clay's startled glance brought her laughter. Wry and rejecting, Clay said, "Travis is all I'm thinking about."

Sobering, she said, "And the man may kill you."

The thought had its weight as Clay remembered the wide-shouldered, aggressive man whose flinty stare had challenged him in the Kilgore kitchen. They rode in silence until Consuela Markham said, "This is the straight way to Cow Springs, one of the last waterholes on my land. Travis must be there."

Clay spurred his horse on.

Ridges cut by draws lay north of them when Consuela Markham's small black-gloved hand pointed that way. Her still-young face flashed humor at him again. "You see, already?"

Clay saw, and ruefully wished this was not on him now. No mistaking the small straw sombrero and slim figure riding to intercept them. There was a chance, Clay hoped, that Patricia Kilgore would have some news for them. The fast, quirted run of her horse suggested that she must have.

22

Travis yanked his hat brim down against the glare of the hot yellow sun as he rode west with Grady Doyle. His long face was impassive, but the strain inside him tightened into driving anger.

Only hours left now to save the future. His impatience to corner the stranger named Clay Mara drove him faster until Doyle called a warning.

"These hosses won't last, runnin' like this!"

Travis pulled down the pace.

They were threading timbered hills, and rode by a cinder cone some hundreds of feet high, covered with a scrub growth and pine almost to the top.

They skirted lava sheets and finally a lava flow, raw, dark and baking in the hot afternoon sunlight as the flow swung left into a winding valley between timbered ridges. Travis led the way beside the flow, thinking of what he had to do. It was simple enough. Get rid of the stranger named Mara; kill the fellow before Patricia and Matt Kilgore saw him again.

Doyle said, "I knowed a man who gave a posse the slip by crossing lava. Only he run into glass lava. It cut the hoofs off his hoss and nigh the boots off his feet when he walked out. He never went near lava again."

Travis made no comment. He was reminding himself that he owned half the Kilgore ranch now. He had all the money and the journal and papers of Roger Travis. He was like a son to Matt Kilgore.

Once Mara was dead, everything could be smoothed

over. . . . And armed men were hunting Mara. Travis knew that after he reached the Kilgore house, he could keep Mara away from Patricia and Matt with a gun. He felt increasingly confident as he eyed the lava flow bulking ten feet and higher at their right.

"The Piedras wagon ruts cross this flow about three miles ahead," Travis said. "We'll cross there. Then you ride to that line cabin and see if your men are back."

"And then what?" Doyle countered.

"Find Mara and shoot him," said Travis curtly. "And you can stay drunk for months on what it's worth to you."

Some minutes later he pulled up sharply, looking back, listening. Doyle swung his horse, listening, too. Spaced gunshots, three shots, like a signal, were reaching across the tumbled lava flow and echoing between the timbered ridges siding the half-mile-wide valley.

Travis caught binoculars from the leather case on his saddle. Two more shots echoed again as he focused on the opposite ridge. He held his voice level as he lowered the glasses.

"Signaling me. Get on to the line cabin. I'll wait here."

Doyle's swollen eye still squinted as he stared curiously. "Who is it?"

"Get going! This is my business!"

Not until Doyle rode on did Travis swing his horse back up the valley. Matt Kilgore also carried binoculars, and Matt had sighted them from the opposite ridge and signaled. Travis wanted no witnesses now, certainly not Grady Doyle.

At the only spot in some distance where the side of the lava flow was broken down, he dismounted and lighted a cigar, and bent the dead match absently between his fingers as he waited.

Matt Kilgore had to lead his horse across the lava. The hesitant strike of shod hoofs on the gas-pocked rock finally became audible. Then Matt's broad-chested figure with vest sagging open as usual appeared at the edge of the lava.

"I almost didn't hear you!" Travis called.

Matt said nothing. With care, he led his horse along the lava edge, and then, slipping and clashing, down the broken side of the flow. The stern look on his face increased the

142

strain in Travis as Matt dropped the reins and spoke harshly.

"I heerd you'd gone to Cow Springs. Who'n hell told you to fence Markham water?"

Guardedly Travis asked, "Have you seen Patricia?"

He felt confident again when Matt said, "Ain't seen her today." Stern temper backed Matt's measured words. "Gid Markham's mother was waitin' at the house for me. Who give you any go-ahead to fence Markham waterholes?"

"Matt, it was the only thing to do," Travis said reasonably. "My lawyer, Jim Rapburn, examined the records in the County Treasurer's office in Socorro and found that the Markhams had no color of title to most of what they claim. Rapburn located the land they've paid taxes on and hold title to. I've had surveys run and found the land which is open. Men are filing on the good water now and will sell to us later."

Flatly Matt said, "We never planned to take any Markham holdings."

With mild injury, Travis said, "I planned it for all of us, Matt. For you, Patricia and me. Sort of a surprise."

Matt's stern temper softened as he pulled off his hat and shoved fingers through his shock of gray hair. "Son, you oughta told me. Now it's an all-fired mess."

Travis was earnest. "The Markhams never were friends."

"They ain't been," Matt agreed. After a moment, he added, "I guess you can't be blamed too much."

Travis relaxed further. The bond between Matt and himself was as strong as ever. He could handle Matt.

"I thought it would please you," Travis said.

"Son, it just don't. Connie Markham owns most of that ranch now. I give Connie my promise there'd be no more trouble. We got to get the men off her land quick."

"I've planned too carefully for that," said Travis calmly.

Matt's stare was quizzical.

"Now ain't that a hell of an argument?" Matt said. He turned to his horse and mounted, and from the saddle spoke calmly. "Son, I've always given orders in this family. And I always keep my word. I gave Connie Markham my promise there won't be trouble again between our families."

Smiling, Travis reminded, "I made no promise."

143

Matt's rope-scarred hand tilted his hat against the sun, giving him a vigorous, younger look.

"Young fellers fulla beans an' ideas is bound to make mistakes," said Matt with blunt coolness. "Like you hirin' that horsethief Doyle and then lettin' him go. And now this grabbin' at Connie Markham's land." A flat roughness entered Matt's tone. "But when a lady looks me in the face and says in cold truth I've lied to her, the mistakes get hobbled and throwed damn quick!"

Matt's stubbornness drove Travis into scorn. "That old woman should have tried being friendly years ago!"

"Old woman?" Matt said. He sat motionless in the saddle, the knotted reins forgotten in his hand as he looked above Travis's head into distance and memories. "A lot of years," Matt said under his breath. "But she'll never be old." His creased face hardened in a way Travis had never seen in Matt before. "Hear me," Matt said. "Every man off Markham land quick!"

In thinning temper, Travis reminded, "I'm half-owner, Matt. Stop talking like I'm a wet-eared brat!"

"Ain't you actin' like one?" cried Matt harshly. "Hear me again! I'm half-owner, too. And I'm runnin' this family like I've always done. Now I'm takin' charge of this mess! I'll get the men off Connie Markham's land. And after this I'll decide what we do."

"Matt!" It broke thickly from Travis at the old man who was suddenly rock-hard, inflexible, like a complete stranger. "I like you, Matt. But don't block me like this. I know what I'm doing. Let me handle everything!" In a kind of breaking fury as the future faced disaster from Matt's stubbornness, Travis cried at him, "Matt! Don't make me!"

"I'll always make you do the right thing!" said Matt sternly.

And Travis realized the truth now. Matt Kilgore was the sort of man who would listen closely to Mara's story. Matt was a stern, just man who would investigate Patricia's suspicions. Matt never could be handled.

With wild temper, knowing suddenly that this was the only way, Travis caught for his gun. And the stricken knowledge of what was coming filled Matt's eyes.

144

Matt half-choked, *"An' I thought I had a son!"* His hand wrenched desperately at the reins.

The words hit Travis like a blow, reminding him of how close he had become to Matt. He hesitated, cocked gun in his hand while the enormity of what he was doing made his hand tremble uncontrollably.

Matt's half-rearing horse was whirling at him and Travis numbly followed instinct—it was either Matt or disaster. Travis jumped back from the horse and fired blindly, twice, at the tall old man in the saddle.

Matt pitched out of the saddle.

Travis stood in shock staring at the sprawled, oddly shrunken figure on the ground. Matt's hat had fallen off. The seed heads of the tawny wild bunch grass brushed Matt's head, making his shock of hair suddenly seem white and lifeless.

"Matt," Travis said thickly. He holstered the smoking gun and spoke louder. "Matt! Why'd you make me, Matt?" And, as Travis turned, almost running to his horse, the last words he would ever hear from Matt were ringing in his ears: *I thought I had a son!*

Travis spurred down the valley without looking back, riding into empty loneliness. He had destroyed something, Travis vaguely sensed, which he would never have again. Once more he was alone. . . . Now only himself mattered, and the future he had planned. To secure that, he had to destroy Clay Mara, and do it swiftly.

Riding fast down the twisting valley, with the sullen flow of black lava close at his right and brush-dotted ridge slope at his left, Travis swore with new anger as he sighted Grady Doyle's burly figure spurring back to meet him.

Doyle's warning was urgent. "They's a bunch of riders comin' from Piedras way. Too many to be our men. Bound to be Markham men!"

A flash of jeering knowledge touched Travis. Driven by the furious urge to destroy Mara, he had scattered his own crew so widely that they could be no help now against a Markham bunch.

Travis forced himself to be calm. "Did they see you?"

"I don't think so," Doyle said. "But quick now they'll

hit the lava back there, where they c'n look this way an' see us!" A twisted grin touched Doyle's mouth as he looked past Travis. "I heerd shots. Whyn't you kill his hoss, too?"

Shock again struck Travis when he looked back up the valley. Matt's gray horse was skirting the lava in a trot after him. The looped reins dropping from Matt's hand had snagged on the saddle horn, and the frightened horse had left the dead for the living. A wildly improbable thought struck Travis that Matt must still be on the horse, following him.

"How close are the men?" Travis demanded.

"Too close! Ain't time to fool with that hoss. Me, I'm gettin' out of sight fast!"

Doyle swung his horse to the ridge slope and spurred up toward the first brush and screening trees. Travis hesitated and followed. The brush slapped at his legs and he fought the feeling of loneliness. On the crest of the ridge, among screening trees, he wheeled his horse alongside Grady Doyle who had pulled up.

In silence they waited watchfully, looking down, while three riders came fast along the valley from the Piedras road and pulled up beside Matt Kilgore's horse. Gid Markham was one of them. He led the men on up the valley, taking Matt's horse.

Doyle spoke under his breath. "They mean to find out what happened."

"Then they can explain it," said Travis. The thought had come at first sight of Markham. When Matt's body was brought in, Gid Markham would be blamed. Who would believe differently? Markham and his crew had been hunting Matt with guns and rage—and now they had him dead as they had planned.

"Wasn't that Kilgore's gray hoss?" Doyle muttered uneasily.

"You didn't see any gray horse," said Travis evenly. "You don't know anything."

Grady Doyle turned a furtive glance. He moistened his lips and nodded.

Travis said, "We'll cross the Piedras road behind Markham's crew, and circle south around them." And mildly he added, "Lead off. I'll follow you."

The unease which struck Grady Doyle was visible. "No need," Doyle muttered. "I'll side you." And, as he swung his horse, Doyle watched Travis from the corner of his eye.

They rode down the far side of the ridge that way, side by side, each aware of the other now. But, for the time being, Travis was careless about it. He was thinking that, with Matt's death fastened on Gid Markham, luck was finally running with him. Only Patricia was left. She would be alone and grieving, and could be handled easily enough now.

Clay held his horse waiting beside Consuela Markham's horse while Patricia brought her lathered roan to a swinging halt alongside them.

"Who are you?" her tight voice threw at him.

Mildly, Clay answered, "I guess I'm the man you seem to think I am."

"Dick's partner?"

"Yes."

"Did you kill Dick?" She was pale.

"That," continued Clay calmly, "is foolish. It happened about like you've heard. Only I went off the trail too."

She was still unbelieving. "Which finger of Dick's left hand was missing?"

Clay's chuckle came. "Dick had all his fingers. You know it."

Still Patricia watched him. "Once," her tight voice said, "you watched the sun rise, and you said something to the person who was with you—"

Clay's gaze cooled. "In Wyoming one morning," he said evenly, "my wife and I watched the sun rise. I told her that she was my sun, never setting, and I wrote it in my journal that night. You've been rummaging like a pack rat in my private life also, I see."

Patricia's suspicions drained away, leaving her face young and defenseless and miserable.

"I remembered that Dick's last letter said his partner had gray eyes and brown hair. Roger didn't have them, and in his room I found the journal and read it. I was afraid."

After a moment the small sad edge of Clay's smile came.

147

"Forgiven," he said. "Does Travis suspect that you know all this?"

Tightness entered Patricia's voice again. "I found Roger at Cow Springs. He denied everything, of course. But now he'll be desperate. Is Dad at the house?"

Clay looked at Consuela Markham. Abrupt fear was in her eyes.

"Well," Clay said. The ominous tone of the word deepened Patricia's pallor. "It had to come," said Clay. He was swinging his horse and talking to Consuela Markham at the same time. "You two will hamper me, ma'am. On the way back to the house, you can tell Patricia how it is."

Her barest nod agreed. Clay lifted the black gelding's trot into a long-striding run on the faint trail Matt Kilgore's horse had made.

When the country roughened and Kilgore's trail pitched down a timbered slope to a sullen flow of black lava almost filling the floor of a small valley, Clay softly whistled. A man like Matt Kilgore who knew the country, could have found a better way than crossing this treacherous lava. But Matt had crossed.

Clay followed, leading the gelding clashing up the broken edge of the lava. On the tumbled surface of the flow, dust had lodged in crevices and depressions, and weeds, grass, scrubby brush and small trees had rooted.

The shod hoofs of Kilgore's horse had left marks which Clay followed, leading the cautiously stepping black gelding. When Clay finally glanced back he abruptly halted.

Through shimmering heat waves over the lava, the woman who was leading a horse after him looked slender and composed. The hot sun caught challenging red tints under her plain straw hat, and Clay waited in quiet temper.

When she reached him, he reminded, "I told you to stay back at the Kilgore house!"

Dorothy Strance tucked in a hair end. "I don't get out a newspaper, Mr. Mara, by waiting in someone's house while important things are happening."

"This matter isn't for a woman!"

Her glance was cool.

"I've told you, Mr. Mara, that I do what I please and

148

print what I please. When the *Beacon* publishes this story, it intends to say exactly who the thief from San Francisco is. And what happens to him."

"The *Beacon*," said Clay shortly, "should be paddled and locked in her office."

The *Beacon* flushed. "I wouldn't attempt it, Mr. Mara. Go about your business. I'll attend to mine."

"Keep back then, out of the way, where you'll be safe."

Clay moved on in some frustration, aware that the *Beacon*, calm and redheaded, was not far behind. . . . And he was not a hundred yards from the edge of the lava flow when he heard a voice ahead.

23

Clay turned back and caught the carbine from the saddle boot and advanced quietly. At the edge of the flow he said, "Easy there!" And not one of the three men below him moved after sighting the carbine. In quiet anger, Clay said, "Well, Markham, so you finally did it?"

Gid Markham, kneeling down there beside Matt Kilgore's body, looked up with visible regret.

"I found his horse down the valley and backtracked to this," Markham said shortly.

The quick steps of Dorothy Strance brought her to the body. "Gid! Gid! What have you done?" she said brokenly.

Markham stood up, anger darkening his thin face. "The man got what he asked for, Dot! I only wish I'd done it!"

"You wish!" she cried. "Gid, send your men out of earshot, or you'll regret it!"

As the two men moved back to the waiting horses, Clay listened intently to Dorothy Strance.

"Someone, Gid, should clear the dead cats and black thinking out of your mind! You're proud of the way you hate the Kilgores, aren't you?"

"Proud?" He shrugged.

"Listen to me, Gid, and don't ask me how I know," she said. "Amos Markham had the idiotic conviction that Matt Kilgore was your father. It turned him against your mother and he built his hate into you."

Gid Markham stared at her. "What a thing to tell a man, Dot!"

"Amos Markham was wrong. He believed a lie! But it warped his life and it's warped yours."

Markham's gaze went to the motionless figure at his feet. "Did Kilgore know this?"

"I'm sure not."

"My mother never mentioned it."

"She never answered your father about it."

"She wouldn't," he said weakly. "Her Rivera pride." After a moment, he added, "But I think she must have taught me the answer when I was small. . . . Be too proud to deny a lie, and always proud enough to admit the truth."

"Yes," Dorothy Strance said.

Gid gestured the matter away as no longer of consequence. He spoke of Matt Kilgore.

"He was on his horse, I think, and the other man shot up at him. One bullet hit the buckle of his shell belt and tore up along his ribs. Another bullet grooved his head. He may have a chance."

"Is he alive?"

"Barely."

"And you're not helping him?" She knelt beside Matt Kilgore.

Gid spoke to Clay. "I've sent men for a wagon and the doctor. There's not much else to do."

"I tracked him across the lava," Clay said. "What other sign is around?"

Markham looked surprised. "Two men rode down the valley here beside the lava. I thought Kilgore was one of them."

"He met the two men," Clay said. He walked past Kilgore and picked up two sets of horse tracks and followed them back. And he heard Gid Markham speaking with wry bluntness to Dorothy Strance.

150

"Dot, a man wouldn't have much peace around you."

"As much as he'd deserve, probably," she said coolly. "But you've never been in any danger, Gid. Hand me your bandanna."

Clay walked slowly around the spot, sorting out the trampled sign. He picked up a dead match and eyed it closely. When he walked back to Dorothy Strance, she had opened Kilgore's shirt and was working on his wounded side.

Clay said, "Give this match to Patricia. It might mean something to her." The match was snapped over in the middle. "I saw Travis light a cigar the other day and break the match like this."

He walked up on the lava flow and led their two horses down. When he started to mount the black gelding, Dorothy Strance came to him.

"Where are you going, Mr. Mara?"

With a touch of malice, Clay reminded, "You print everything that happens. Read your paper for news of this." And levelly he warned, "Don't follow me this time, or you will sit painful tomorrow."

She said coldly, "I believe you really would."

"Just try me, ma'am."

"You're going after Travis." She was earnest. "The sheriff should do that. Or Gid has men waiting at the road."

Clay settled in the saddle and looked thoughtfully down at her as he gathered the reins.

"The sheriff, ma'am, is a hundred and fifty miles away. Markham's gunmen would shoot Travis on sight."

"And what, Mr. Mara, will you do?"

Clay's faint smile lacked humor. "I won't kiss him."

"Travis will try to kill you!" And when Clay said nothing, she gazed up at him uncertainly, looking for a moment like a slightly older copy of her small distressed daughter in the sandpile. "Matt needs me here. And Patricia will need you, Mr. Mara. Is this risk necessary?"

"It is," Clay said, and touched a spur and left her standing there.

Between the lava and the ridge slope, old tracks and new tracks cut the earth. The Markham horses had trampled the sign Clay followed. He angled over to the base of the slope and advanced there, watching the ground. When he cut fresh prints of shod horses leading up the ridge slope, he studied them a moment, drew the carbine and followed the sign.

Brush raked his legs. The click and scuff of his gelding's hoofs sounded loud in the quiet as trees closed around. Clay pulled up where trampled prints showed two riders had paused and looked back down into the valley. They had watched Gid Markham pass down there, of course, and then the two men had ridden on across the ridge crest. Clay shook the gelding into a run after them.

When Travis and Doyle rode cautiously and quickly across the Piedras road, the waiting Markham riders were bunched in the distance at the black lava. Beyond the road, screening pines and cedars closed in and Travis said, "We'll swing south around them."

"There's lava that way," Doyle reminded.

"I crossed that lava once with Matt Kilgore," said Travis confidently. "Matt followed cattle and deer trails."

The mention of Matt Kilgore prodded the empty feeling of loss in Travis as they advanced into roughening country, with lava outcropping increasing among the scrub pines and cedars. On a low ridge, Travis used the binoculars to scan the country behind them, and his sideward glance caught Doyle's furtive uneasiness on him.

"We'll take the first good trail west," Travis said as he cased the glasses.

Doyle rode with him in silence. The trail they found and followed held cattle and horse tracks and deer sign. As they advanced, older lava was buried under more recent flows, many of the flows raw and open, the lava tumbled, twisted, broken. Increasingly the landscape took on an awesome aspect from the ancient eruptions frozen in mid-fury.

Travis rode in silence also, planning coolly, like a gambler in a high, dangerous game which he meant to win, no matter how he had to play.

Matt Kilgore's death, he was confident, would be blamed on Gid Markham.

But if something happened to that hope, then Grady

152

Doyle could take the blame for shooting Matt. Doyle would not be alive to deny it; by sundown Doyle would be dead because Doyle was treacherous and dangerous.

That left only the stranger named Clay Mara. And with Mara dead no threat at all would be left, Travis was confident.

He and Patricia would own the Kilgore ranch. Patricia would be lonely and grieving, but any doubts which persisted in her could be talked away. With the strong feeling of recklessly gambling in a game he was determined to win, Travis already had decided on the move which would appease Patricia. He turned his head as Grady Doyle lifted his voice.

"You still goin' to the Kilgore house?" Doyle inquired.

"Yes."

"Markham'll be there quick with his men."

"I'll be there first," Travis said. And his slight smile came as he spoke of the change in his plans which would disarm much of Patricia's suspicion, add blame to the Markhams, and free every effort to find Mara.

"Miss Kilgore," Travis said, "asked me to pull the men off the Markham waterholes. I want to tell her I'm doing that. Then I'll saddle a fresh horse and ride on to get our men together." Travis added, "If Matt Kilgore isn't at the house, I'll find him and tell him."

He saw the incredulous look Grady Doyle gave him and ignored it. Still planning ahead he was thinking with some amusement that the water rights were still legally filed. They could safely wait until pressure eased off.

"Faster!" Travis said. "I've got to reach the house before Markham's men."

The trail they were following crossed open sheets of lava and followed defiles and reaches between the lava flows where mats of green grass grew. Little-used trails split off. Travis kept Doyle's burly figure in the corner of his eye. Doyle seemed to sense it. A pale sheen of perspiration began to show on Doyle's meaty face.

Coolly Travis watched Doyle's growing fear. He had no feeling at all about what was going to happen to Doyle.

153

"Matt Kilgore claims the cattle hunt these pockets of good grass back in here," Travis said. "It's sweeter, richer grass."

"I reckon," Doyle said. His voice had a strained sound.

The sun was dropping to the horizon. Shadows were reaching out. Travis said again, "Faster!"

They rode through a long defile between high masses of lava, and the defile opened into a broad expanse of green grass where scattered cattle and a bull broke away from their advance.

"They're carrying my brand," Travis noticed.

Doyle wet his lips and was silent as they followed the trail to the end of the grass, where a small pond of greenish blue water reflected a white cloud overhead.

Travis pulled up, staring at hoof-churned mud around the water and the high raw lava beyond. He looked around the parklike expanse of grass which was walled all around, he saw now, with lava.

Travis's temper suddenly flared. "No way out of here but the way we came in. The trail headed here to water and grass!"

"A man can get lost in this lava," Doyle said uneasily.

"We'll backtrack and find a way through," said Travis, with new harshness. He wrenched his horse around, and the feeling that luck was running against him made his temper corrosive and dangerous.

Some miles south of the Piedras road, the horse tracks which Clay Mara was following turned into a cattle trail and held to it. He was gaining, Clay guessed, and pressed the gelding faster.

The landscape took on a desolate look as he entered the lava beds. He was riding west and pulled his hat brim lower against the full blaze of the setting sun. Lengthening shadows gave a sullen unreality to the increasing masses of raw lava. The sense of being alone in a frozen world of past cataclysms became stronger. Men could be shot down in these wild, lonely lava stretches and not be found. The fresh hoof marks reaching ahead sharpened the knowledge that the two men ahead would kill on sight. He rode now with the carbine across his lap, ready.

Travis seemed to be swinging around the Markham crew, heading west toward the Kilgore house. Travis must have some plan; he must believe that Matt Kilgore was dead, and be confident. Squinting into the dazzling glare of the sun, Clay rode through another defile between the endless flows. And suddenly, out of the blaze of the setting sun, a mass of cattle charged through the defile right at him, it seemed.

The gelding snorted and halted, then acted by instinct.

Whirling, it took to the lava. Stumbling, recovering, haunches driving, the horse scrambled up the steep, treacherous footing. And the steers bolted past just behind them in a slamming mass of horns and flesh.

Through the tumult and dust came muffled gunshots as the gelding topped the edge of the flow. It half-reared and fell as Clay kicked the stirrups away and twisted out of the saddle, holding to the carbine.

In the sun glare, he made out two riders in the defile. They had sighted him riding up against the skyline and had fired instantly.

Clay stumbled over the rough lava away from the horse and whipped up the carbine. He forced himself to be steady because this shot had to count. And, when he squeezed the trigger, he brought the first horse down. The rider launched off safely. A quick second shot missed him.

Both the riders were afoot now, ducking up the steep slope behind huge slabs of lava rock. Before they disappeared, Clay was running at them.

The lava through here had a scorched, reddish hue, like vast chunks of cinder, honeycombed with gas bubbles. Some of it had weathered, crumbled. The jagged fragments ground under Clay's boots as he ran forward. Immense broken slabs forced him into reckless leaps.

A bullet shrilled past his shoulder, and the long face of Travis appeared at the side of a massive lava block. Clay fired. Dust spurted off the block. The figure which appeared behind Travis was the burly man named Doyle.

Now Clay knew what he faced. He went down on the

flow, and the sharp lava bruised his hands as he scrambled forward. Closing in on them fast was the only way. Otherwise, they'd box him and pick him off.

Clay heard them shooting. Then they waited, trying, evidently, to sight him as he advanced. He risked a look and nothing happened. He stood up and, when the two men still stayed down out of sight, ran directly at the large, tilted slab of gas-pocked lava where he had last sighted them.

He was at the slab before he sighted Doyle down in the defile again, starting a rein-slashing retreat on the one horse that was left. Clay used a corner of the tilted slab to steady the carbine. Again he forced himself to be calm before he gently squeezed the trigger.

It was good enough. When he stepped around the lava slab, Travis lay there, face up, coat and shirt open, hands groping aimlessly for a gun that was not there.

Clay left the helpless man there and went to Grady Doyle, sprawled motionless down in the defile. The horse, its reins dragging, was sidling away. Clay led the horse back.

A soft leather money belt dangled half out of Doyle's coat pocket and explained why Travis's shirt had been ripped open.

When Clay opened the money belt, he whistled softly. The pockets of the belt were stuffed with currency of large denomination and deposit certificates on St. Louis banks made out to Roger Travis. The man had been carrying much of the money he had gotten from the South Bay Bank in San Francisco. And Doyle had almost escaped with it.

When Clay returned to Travis, the man was breathing with deep effort.

"Get him?" Travis mumbled.

"He's dead," Clay said.

"Couldn't watch him an' you, too," Travis whispered. "He knew I meant to shut his mouth."

"Because of Matt Kilgore?" Clay guessed.

"Mostly," Travis said thinly. The first cool shadows were reaching across Travis. He shivered. Eyes rolled to the raw, forbidding lava all around, and closed. "Lonesome here," Travis got out with effort. "Don't leave me." Pink bubbled on his lips.

156

Clay went to a knee, and lifted the kerchief folds from Travis's neck and wiped the bubbles away. "I'm with you," Clay said.

"Shot me in the back twice," mumbled Travis with effort. He breathed shallowly, rapidly, and then said, "Tell the *padre*."

Travis knew that he was dying, Clay saw. "Want the *padre* to say prayers?" Clay suggested.

Something close to humor entered Travis's clouding gaze.

"The *padre's* said the prayers already," Travis said weakly. "Told me they weren't wasted. He'll understand."

"I'll tell him."

Travis's breathing was again quick and shallow before he gained strength to smile wanly. "Thought you were dead," he whispered. "Seemed like a good gamble."

"It was," Clay agreed.

Travis sighed softly. "I thought I'd found everything here that we lost in Wyoming."

"We?" Clay said.

Looking down at the long-boned face, going gray, it came to Clay how deeply this man must have entered into another man's life.

"All here," said Travis faintly. "Guess I tried for too much." He struggled for breath and sought Clay's face. "Hated it about Matt. . . . I liked Matt. Wish I hadn't shot him."

"Kilgore's got a chance to live," Clay said.

Slowly Travis's eyes closed. "Good!" he said weakly. The graying face seemed peaceful now.

Hours later, when Clay rode Grady Doyle's weary horse into the yellow lamplight streaming from the Kilgore kitchen windows and open back door, he was still thinking about Travis with a strange lack of animosity.

The feeling stayed with him as he talked out back of the house with a relieved Howie Quist and Ira Bell, and watched Gid Markham take his crew to bring in Travis and Doyle.

Doctor Paul Halvord had reached the house some time ago. Matt Kilgore was in his own bed. And one had only to look at Consuela Markham's face, bright with an inner singing, to know that Kilgore was doing all right.

The lamplit kitchen, warm from the big iron range, held an extra glow and warmth, it seemed to Clay as he took the mug of hot coffee which the Widow Strance poured for him.

"In a few minutes, we'll have something for you to eat," she told him.

He was weary, dirty, and hungry but Clay smiled. "No hurry," he said. A moment later Patricia Kilgore came into the kitchen. Clay looked at her still strained pallor and hesitated before he said, "You might like to know that Travis was sorry about what happened. He thought a lot of your father."

"He showed it," said Patricia. She was bitter.

Clay tried to explain. "Travis was a gambler. His game was big here. But when he lost, he took it like a gambler."

"It's a little something to remember about him," Patricia said. "He—" She bit her lip, turned abruptly and left the kitchen again, looking young and shaken.

Gazing after her, Clay guessed that with Matt Kilgore doing well her laughter and zest would soon be back. Then he became aware of Consuela Markham at the sink, holding a dishtowel, trim and remarkably youthful looking in a gay print apron. She was watching him. The amused knowledge of an older woman was in her eyes and in her question.

"Patricia is so pretty tonight, isn't she?"

Clay took a swallow of coffee and grinned. "Mighty pretty. She'll make some man a fine wife."

"Soon?" asked Consuela Markham with amusement.

"Not too long now, I'd say," Clay guessed.

Dorothy Strance was setting his place at the kitchen table. She was thoughtful. "It will seem strange to call you Mr. Travis."

"You'll get used to it," Clay said.

"Now that you've recovered a good part of your money, and since most of the rest is in your half interest in the ranch, do you intend to settle down here?"

"Still prying, ma'am?"

Color flushed her smooth cheeks. "I have to print this story."

Consuela Markham said, "Did you see how he looked at Patricia? I think we can guess what Mr. Mara intends to do. . . . Now, Dorothy, if some good man would just take you in hand."

"She needs it," Clay drawled.

Dorothy flushed and moved the plate on the checked tablecloth. "Such talk isn't necessary."

"If ever a young lady," Clay said, "needed a good man to take her in hand. I could—"

"I think this is enough of such talk," said the widow firmly. Her face was fiery as she moved to the open back door.

Her plain dress and bright red hair pinned back only made more obvious, Clay thought, the slenderness of her figure and the softness of her face. In this moment, she looked once more like her small distressed daughter.

Clay watched her across his lifted coffee mug. "Ma'am, if I really try—"

From the doorway, the Widow Strance eyed his grin in unbelief and said, "I believe you really would try, Mr. Mara." And, when Clay's grin widened, she said, "I've heard enough!"

"Ma'am," Clay said, "you haven't started to hear."

He put the mug on the table and started toward her. She looked wildly at Consuela Markham and found no help there. Something like panic caught her.

"I knew you were dangerous, Mr. Mara! But—" She watched Clay coming on and fled suddenly out into the night.

Clay paused in the doorway, giving a promise which satisfied even Consuela Markham's fascinated gaze.

"You'll read all about it in her newspaper, ma'am."

And then, knowing now beyond all doubt that a man without bold plans and high hopes had nothing, really, Clay followed the Widow Strance out into the night.

T. T. Flynn was born Thomas Theodore Flynn, Jr., in Indianapolis, Indiana. He was the author of over a hundred Western short novels for such leading pulp magazines as Street and Smith's *Western Story Magazine*, Popular Publications' *Dime Western*, and Dell's *Zane Grey's Western Magazine*. His short novel *Hell's Half Acre* appeared in the issue which launched *Star Western* in 1933. He moved to New Mexico with his wife Helen and spent much of his time living in a trailer while on the road exploring the vast terrain of the American West. His descriptions of the land are always detailed, but he used them not only for local color but also to reflect the heightening of emotional distress among the characters within a story. Following the Second World War, Flynn turned his attention to the book-length Western novel and in this form also produced work that has proven imperishable. Five of these novels first appeared as original paperbacks, most notably *The Man From Laramie* which was featured as a serial in *The Saturday Evening Post* and subsequently made into a memorable motion picture directed by Anthony Mann and starring James Stewart. *Two Faces West*, which deals with the problems of identity and reality, served as the basis for a television series. He was highly innovative and inventive and in later novels, such as *Riding High*, concentrated on deeper psychological issues as the source for conflict, rather than more elemental motives like greed. He was so meticulous about his research that he once spent days to determine the exact year that blue- (as opposed to red-) checked tablecloths were introduced because all anachronism was anathema to him. Flynn is at his best in stories which combine mystery — not surprisingly, he also wrote detective fiction — suspense, and action in an artful balance. The world in which his characters live is often a comedy of errors in which the first step in any direction frequently can, and does, lead to ever deepening complications. His most recent books have been *Night of the Comanche Moon, Rawhide: A Western Quintet*, and *Long Journey to Deep Cañon: A Western Quartet*.

New
PA

T^{λ}

0 3 APR 2017